Davey had one goal in mind when he joined the mutants — enter every lab he possibly could and find his best friend. Evan has been missing for years, but Davey never lost hope he would find him. He has to, because it's his fault Evan ended up in a cage.

Orion only ever wanted a peaceful life, but instead, he was forced to be a hunter. Now he finally has a chance at the life he dreamed of, and he'll cling to it with both hands.

When Davey bursts into Orion's bakery to save him from burning cookies, he doesn't expect to meet his mate. He's not quite sure what to do with Orion when his focus should be on finding Evan, but maybe he can let go of his guilt and give himself and Orion a chance to be happy.

He and Orion might lose each other if he can't.

This book is a work of fiction. Names, characters, places, and incidents either are products of the author's imagination or are used fictitiously. Any resemblance to actual events or locales or persons, living or dead, is entirely coincidental.

Davey
Copyright © 2024 Catherine Lievens
ISBN: 978-1-4874-4237-8
Cover art by Angela Waters

Published by eXtasy Books Inc

Look for us online at:
www.eXtasybooks.com

Davey
Mutants 6

By

Catherine Lievens

CHAPTER ONE

"Is everyone ready?" Moore asked, looking at the people gathered around him.

Davey ignored him. Moore always checked if everyone was ready before they left, which was ridiculous because they knew what to expect. Of course they were ready. They'd been raiding labs and saving people for a while now.

Davey swallowed and bounced on the balls of his feet. He was more than ready to go, but he had to wait for Moore to give the signal. As soon as Moore did, Davey turned to Teddy, who held out a hand and rolled his eyes.

"I don't get why you're always so eager to go," he said as others touched him.

"Why wouldn't I be? The labs shouldn't exist, and we're taking them down one by one. I don't know about you, but it's the perfect job for me, and I take great pleasure in making sure those doctors won't hurt anyone ever again."

Teddy didn't look convinced, but there wasn't time for them to talk. As soon as everyone was touching him, he shimmered them away, and the raid was on.

They couldn't afford to be distracted, which was good because Davey didn't want anyone to start asking questions. He wasn't ready for people to find out why he was always so eager to go on raids. He didn't know how Moore would react if he did, and he needed to do this.

He stepped away from Teddy once they landed because he wanted to avoid more questions, and he huddled close to Olga instead. She glanced his way and arched a brow.

Maybe he shouldn't have chosen her.

"What do you know?" he asked her.

"Who says I know anything?"

"You see the future."

"I don't see *all* the future."

"No, but you have *that* face, and I know you know something."

She grinned. "Do I?"

She was infuriating. She saw the future, but as far as Davey knew, she'd never been able to control that power. She saw whatever the universe wanted her to see, so it probably had nothing to do with him.

But it also could have everything to do with him.

There was no way for Davey to know, and he wasn't sure he wanted to. Olga was secretive about the things she saw. She always said that she didn't want anyone to do things differently just because of what she saw, especially when it came to their private lives. As far as Davey was concerned, he didn't want to know if anything she saw involved him. He didn't even want to know if she saw his mate, because he wasn't ready to meet whoever that was. Maybe he never would be.

He definitely didn't want to meet his mate before he managed to rescue Evan.

He swallowed and took a careful step away. Olga snickered, but Davey ignored her. That was made easier by Moore getting everyone's attention and the small crowd around them quieting down.

"You know what to do," Moore said, gesturing at the lab they were standing in front of.

It was hidden between the trees. That had to have been done on purpose, because the only thing that Davey could see was a metal door embedded in the wall. The vegetation covered everything else except for a small white box on the wall by the door.

The alarm system.

That wouldn't be a problem. Matthew stepped up to the door and examined the white box for a moment before pressing two fingers to it. Davey was sure that when the scientists had experimented on them all and had *changed* them, giving them powers they thought they would be able to replicate and exploit, they hadn't expected the mutants to get out of the labs and work against them. Matthew's electricity, Davey's water manipulation, Olga's future seeing—they could have used it for their personal gain, but instead, they were using it to kill as many doctors and scientists as they could.

Davey loved it. It was revenge, but at the same time, he felt like the scientists should have expected it. Did they really think that the people they experimented on would stay in their cages and wait for whatever came next? Hadn't they realized that the people they hurt would eventually want to hurt them? Whatever the case, Davey was happy that he could do all of this. He'd saved himself and countless other people, and even though he hadn't yet saved the most important person, he was sure that eventually, he would.

He just had to find Evan first.

Matthew opened the door and gestured at everyone else to get in. Davey rushed forward, walking into the building right behind Olga. She looked badass in her black uniform, all playfulness gone from her expression. She was laser-focused now, ready to take down whoever stood in her way.

As was Davey.

It always took a while for them to reach the prisoners. They had to take care of the guards first, then of the scientists and anyone else who'd been working here. It always amazed Davey in the worst way that so many people were ready to hurt others for a paycheck.

He rounded a corner and noticed another metal door

embedded in the wall at the end of the hallway. There was a guard standing in front of it, a gun in his hand. He raised it when he saw Davey, but Davey was faster. He reached a hand out and pulled the water from the guard's eyes.

The guard screamed. Before, Davey would have done something much showier, like pulling all the water from the guy's body and turning him into a dry husk. That took quite a bit of power, though, and he wanted to be ready for whatever was behind the door. Taking the fluid out of someone's eyes was just as effective because it meant the guard was blind.

The guard continued screaming, and Davey kicked his knee. The gun clattered on the floor when the guard went down, and while Davey didn't usually use weapons, he picked it up in case someone decided to come around while he was in the room.

The door was locked, but that wasn't a surprise. Davey didn't have Matthew's electricity ability, so instead, he crouched next to the whimpering guard and started going through the man's pockets. He found a badge and pressed it against the white box by the door.

The lock made a loud click when it opened. Davey grinned at himself, pocketed the badge, and opened the door.

The smell hit him first. It was always the same — unwashed bodies, blood, infection, and death. The various labs were slightly different from one another, but the cage rooms were always the same.

It was where the scientists and nurses kept the prisoners. When they needed to hurt them, they picked them up and took them to the operating rooms. When they didn't need them anymore, they returned them to the cages to suffer and sometimes die.

Davey swallowed and stepped in as he slipped the gun into the back pocket of his jeans. He looked around the room, expecting more guards, but there was no one there. That was strange, but maybe the guards had decided to focus on the areas of the facility that were more easily defended. Here, they'd be in danger not only from Davey and his people, but also from the people in the cages.

Most of them were cowering at the back of the cages, barely looking at him. His first instinct was to open them to let them out, but he'd seen what could happen a few times, and he wasn't ready for that. These people deserved to be free, but first, his team would have to ensure they wouldn't attack. Sometimes these poor people lost their minds and mistook Davey and the other mutants for nurses or doctors.

Davey couldn't blame them. He knew what it was like to be in their place.

He walked down the row of cages, keeping an eye on the prisoners. Some of them were naked, while others were in their animal forms. Some wore scrubs, and all of them looked terrified.

A whimper caught his attention. He looked at a cage on his right and stopped moving.

A small figure was bundled up tightly at the back of the cage. The man was wearing scrubs, but beyond his blond hair, that was all Davey could see of him. His shoulders shook, and he was visibly terrified.

"Evan?" Davey called out.

The man in the cage tensed and started to turn. Davey's heart raced as he looked around the cage. The lock didn't have a key but rather a small screen. Davey pressed the badge he'd found on the guard against it, sighing in relief when the door unlocked. He opened it and stepped in, his gaze on Evan.

Who turned and raised a gun.

"What do you think?" Rikar asked.

5

Orion looked around the room. He had his hands on his hips, and he was trying to be serious, but inside, he wanted nothing more than to laugh. His chest bubbled with happiness, something he hadn't felt in too long.

In fact, he couldn't remember ever feeling so happy. It was hard to believe he did, but he was here, in the middle of the village, standing in a closed bakery.

Maybe it wouldn't be closed for much longer.

He grinned at Rikar. "I like it."

"Then it's yours," Rikar said with a smile.

Sometimes, Orion still had a hard time accepting that the village had welcomed him and his brother with open arms. Well, maybe not exactly open arms, but after Perseus and Orion had told them everything they knew about the hunters and their father, they'd become part of the village. Their position had been strengthened when Perseus and Teddy had bonded. They were truly part of this place now, and they weren't going anywhere.

Which was why Orion was thinking about opening his own bakery. It had been a dream of his, but he'd never actually thought he would get to do it. He'd believed he'd be a hunter for the rest of his life and that it wouldn't take him long to die. Hunters seldom lived long, except for a few of them who were smart enough to take a step back when they got hurt.

Orion's father was still alive because he was a coward. He never hesitated to send Orion and Perseus on hunts, but he didn't often go with them. He preferred controlling everything from his couch, which was one of the reasons Orion hated him.

He had a very long list of reasons he hated his father.

"Are you sure?" he asked Rikar because he didn't want to think about his father.

He ignored the way Perseus bumped their shoulders

together and kept his attention on the village leader. He already knew what Perseus was trying to tell him, anyway.

Rikar nodded. "I'm very sure. As you can see, the bakery's been closed for a while. The people who ran it moved away from the village, and we haven't found anyone else who wanted to give it a try. I miss fresh bread."

Orion looked around again. "I don't know if I'll be any good at it. I mean, I've never actually owned a bakery. I love to bake, and I love to eat what I bake, but I don't know how that will translate to opening a bakery."

Rikar grabbed Orion's shoulder and squeezed. "You want to open a bakery, right?"

"Yeah."

Sometimes, it didn't feel real. Orion could hardly believe he was allowed to talk about his dreams and, even more so, to try to make one of them come true.

Opening a bakery had only been one of his dreams. He wanted to find someone to share his life with, to have a family together, and to live a happy life. He supposed it was good that he had at least one of those ready to go. There was still time for the love thing, and even more so for the family.

"Then this is yours. I don't think anyone in the village expects you to be a perfect baker right away. They know you don't have experience, but the few who've tasted your food were very enthusiastic. They can't wait for you to open this place again."

Orion flushed and looked down at his feet. He still had a hard time accepting compliments, especially when they came from people with authority. Perseus had always told Orion that everything he baked was perfect, but he was Orion's brother. He kind of *had* to say that.

But Rikar didn't. The village leader tried to be honest with everyone, and Orion wasn't any different. If Rikar hadn't thought Orion could do it, he wouldn't have offered him the bakery. He wouldn't have mentioned it at all.

"You won't have to do this alone," Perseus murmured, knocking their shoulders together again.

Orion snorted. "Are you going to help me bake?"

Perseus grimaced. "I think I'd probably burn down this place if I tried. I might not be able to help you with the baking, but I can clean. Maybe talk to the people who'll come into the shop."

"You'd scare them right back out," Orion pointed out. "You're grumpy on the best of days and even grumpier when Teddy isn't with you."

Perseus's mate was on a raid today. Orion was curious about what happened during those raids, but not curious enough to ask to go with them. He wasn't a hunter anymore. He never should have been one, but he hadn't had a choice.

Now, he did.

"I won't growl at the customers," Perseus promised. When Orion arched a brow, he quickly added, "Much."

Orion couldn't do this by himself, but he wouldn't have to. His brother wasn't going anywhere, even though he had a mate now. They'd been hunters together, and they'd escaped together. If it weren't for Perseus, Orion would probably be dead right now, but instead, he was here, starting a new life. Perseus would be with him every step of the way, and now Orion also had Teddy and all the other mutants.

Some of them were still wary of him and Perseus, as were some of the people who lived in the village. Orion didn't blame them. He'd be wary of himself, too, even though there was no reason to be. He didn't expect these people to understand that he and his brother had been forced to be hunters by their father. When they were ready to accept Orion and Perseus, they would, and in the meantime, Orion would strive to show them that even though he'd been a hunter, he'd never been a bad person.

He hoped that opening the bakery would help with that. He prayed that people would come in and buy his goods and maybe get to know him. He wasn't going anywhere. That meant opening up to the people who lived here.

Perseus didn't care about all of that, but Orion did, and he wanted more. He wanted to be part of something good, and while he supposed he had been part of something when he was a hunter, that hadn't been good. He wanted to do something good, and this was his opportunity to do so.

"I can't promise I'll be able to do this, but I'll do my best," he told Rikar.

The Nix nodded. He was still smiling, which made Orion think that maybe he believed in him. Perseus had always been the only one who did, so this felt good.

"That's all I'm asking," Rikar said before turning to Perseus. "What about you? Are you serious about working here with Orion, or do I need to find you something else to do?"

Perseus and Orion weren't allowed to go on raids, which was perfectly fine with Orion because he didn't want to. He was eager to help and give the mutants information, but he was done with violence. From now on, his life would be focused on firing up ovens and baking cookies.

"I'll work with Orion, at least initially," Perseus said. "I want to help him establish the bakery, and I think he would have a hard time finding people to work with, considering the situation."

"If you have any kind of trouble with anyone, I want you to tell me. I understand people aren't sure what to think about you, but you're members of this tribe now. Both you and Orion are part of our family, and I take that seriously. I won't allow anyone to hurt you."

"I don't think they'd hurt us physically," Orion said, still glancing around because he couldn't quite believe this place was his. "And I don't blame them. We were hunters, after all."

"With extenuating circumstances, and even then, you've been helping us. You deserve a place here."

Orion suspected it would take him some time to believe that, but that was fine, because he *had* time.

This was his home now. It might feel like a dream, but it wasn't.

Orion was still afraid because he felt like he could never be truly free of his father, but he knew that eventually he'd settle and relax into his new life. In the meantime, he was planning on working as hard as he could to build his future.

Almost dying had been the best thing that could have happened to him.

The gun fired before Davey could do anything. For a few seconds, he felt like nothing had happened. Then something hit him in the shoulder as he stared at the man crouched at the back of the cage.

Not Evan. Never him.

He stumbled back and hit the cage behind him. He still couldn't feel pain, but he knew what had happened now.

He'd been shot.

Someone yelled, and Davey turned toward the door. Moore was rushing in, Leon and Teddy behind him. Davey could relax. They would neutralize the man who'd shot him and ensure he couldn't hurt anyone else.

It wasn't Evan. Once again, Davey hadn't found him.

He slumped against the cage and slowly slid to the floor. Moore ran to the man in the cage. One flicker of Teddy's hand and the gun in the man's hand exploded. The man screamed and stumbled back, holding his hand against his chest.

That had to hurt almost as much as taking a bullet to the shoulder.

Leon knelt next to Davey and reached for Davey's

shoulder. Davey shook his head, not wanting anyone to realize how badly he was hurt. He shouldn't have been in this room on his own. He shouldn't have been on his own at all. When they raided labs, they had to be in pairs. Davey usually managed to get around that rule so he could look for Evan without anyone asking questions, but clearly, this time, he wouldn't be able to hide.

"Let me see that," Leon said as he tore Davey's t-shirt to get a better look at the wound.

Davey whimpered, because it fucking hurt. Leon wasn't being particularly gentle, probably because he wanted to heal the wound as quickly as he could.

Leon helped Davey sit up to check the back of the wound. "It went through, so I don't have to worry about digging the damn thing out," he muttered.

Davey closed his eyes. He trusted Leon with his life. His friend would heal him, and he'd be as good as new in just a few moments.

He kept his eyes closed as the pain slowly faded. He groaned in relief when he could move his shoulder again without wanting to scream, then opened his eyes. "Thank you."

Leon's expression was serious. "You're welcome, but please, don't get shot again."

Davey huffed. "I'll do my best, but I can't make promises."

Leon got to his feet and offered Davey his hand. Davey took it and allowed his friend to haul him to his feet. When he looked at the man who'd shot him, he wasn't surprised to see that Moore was already dragging him out of the cage.

From behind, the man had looked like Evan, but he didn't from the front. There was no kindness in his eyes and no apology on his lips. Evan would never have shot anyone, let alone Davey.

Moore marched the guy down the hallway, ignoring his

begging. Davey watched him go, his stomach churning with anxiousness and fear. He needed to find Evan.

"He's a nurse," Teddy said. "I guess he thought that by hiding in one of the cages, we'd think he was one of the survivors. Someone would have told us that wasn't true, though, so he had to act."

Davey nodded. "Makes sense."

He could feel both Teddy and Leon staring at him, but he ignored them as he walked down the hallway between the cages.

"You were here on your own," Leon said.

"I'm fine."

"Only because I healed you. You wouldn't have been fine if I hadn't been here."

"But you were, and *I'm fine*."

Leon didn't look convinced. Davey didn't have it in him to answer questions, so he ignored him and left the room with the cages. People were rushing in to help the survivors, but he couldn't find it in himself to do it. All his thoughts were focused on Evan and the fact that he wasn't here.

That was all Davey could think about as they explored the facility and poked around. His thoughts were never far from his best friend, but today especially. He really thought he'd found Evan.

He hadn't.

He knew he was in trouble when, once they were back at the village, Moore grabbed his shoulder to stop him from leaving. Together, they watched the others scatter, all of them eager to go home. Davey was, too, but Moore wouldn't let this go, so he might as well not even try to avoid him.

"I'm putting you in timeout," Moore declared.

Davey whipped his head toward him. "What are you talking about?"

"What you did was incredibly dangerous. You shouldn't

have been alone, especially not in that room. You know how some of the survivors react when we reach them. You know some of them are dangerous."

"None of them attacked me."

"No, but you were shot. What would have happened if we hadn't arrived when we did?"

Davey would probably be dead, which meant he wouldn't be able to find his best friend. "I promise I won't do it again. I just wanted to check on them, you know?"

Moore stared for a second before nodding. "I do know, but it's getting too dangerous. I can't trust you not to act on your own, and I'm afraid to trust you with the lives of the other mutants. Until you get your head out of your ass, you're off the raids. You need to take a step back, rethink about why you're doing this, and find a better balance."

"I swear you don't have to do that. It was a one-time thing." Davey couldn't afford to be left behind when there were raids. He was sometimes, because Moore didn't take every mutant with him every time, but Davey could deal with that when he knew that next time, he'd be there.

Mostly.

He always freaked out when he was left behind, and he suspected that Moore had noticed. Why else would he be doing this now?

Moore didn't know what Davey was doing or why it was so vital for him to go on all the raids. He didn't know that because of Davey, Evan was being hurt every day. He didn't know a lot about Davey, and while Davey wasn't planning on telling him any of it, he needed to come up with something that would convince Moore to allow him to go with the others.

But Moore was already shaking his head. "I'm not going to lose you. You're making stupid mistakes, which, to me, points to the fact that you're emotionally involved."

"Aren't we all? I mean, we were all in those cages at one time. How can you not be emotional when you see them?" Davey still had nightmares, and while he knew that the raids weren't making things any easier on him, he wasn't giving up.

"I've seen the way you behave, and I'm not the only one. It's like you're searching for something or maybe someone. Is that what's going on?"

Davey wanted to tell Moore, but he was afraid of what would happen if he did. He fully expected to be kicked out of the village and never be allowed to go on the raids again. He couldn't risk it. No matter how much he wanted to tell Moore and the others about Evan, he couldn't.

"I told you I was fine," he said through gritted teeth. He felt like if he allowed himself to, he would blurt out the entire story.

"You're not, and you haven't been in a long time. I understand it might be because of the labs and everything else, but that's one more reason for you to take a step back. I'm not kicking you off the team or out of the village, so I don't want you to worry about that. I just feel you need to take time off away from the fighting, and that's what I'm offering."

"I don't need to take time off," Davey snapped.

Moore crossed his arms over his chest. "It's non-negotiable. I wasn't asking you if you wanted to do this. I'm telling you it's happening."

Davey could see that nothing he could say would change Moore's mind. He glared at him and stomped away, eager not to see his face again. Moore didn't call him back.

"What happened?" Hansen asked as he fell into step with Davey.

Davey hadn't seen him lurking around, but he should have. "Nothing."

"More like nothing you want to talk about. Don't do

anything stupid, Davey. There's a reason Moore benched you, and going out there on your own isn't going to help. It's going to get you killed, in fact, and no one wants to lose you."

"Just leave me alone," Davey grumbled before speeding away. He didn't start running, but it was a close thing.

He understood why his friends were worried about him. He would feel the same way if one of them was behaving like he was.

But they didn't know the entire story. They didn't know that Davey had to save Evan.

Orion and Perseus were still poking around the bakery when Teddy walked in. Rikar had left a while earlier, promising Orion that everything would be okay and that he would have the support he needed from both Rikar and the tribe. Orion still couldn't believe these people were so willing to help him. Even though he always tried his best never to hurt people, he'd been a hunter. Why weren't these people afraid of him?

He had no doubt that some of them were. He didn't miss the way some tribe members crossed the street when they saw him coming. He wouldn't deny he was intimidating, but they had to know that he wouldn't be here if he was dangerous. They were avoiding him because of who he'd been, and that was fine. It would take time for people to trust that he wouldn't hurt or betray them.

It would take even more time for him to believe he could actually do this.

"This place looks nice," Teddy said as he made a beeline for Perseus.

Perseus grinned at him, and his entire body relaxed. It was something that only happened when Teddy and Orion were around, but Orion hoped that now that Perseus was at peace, he wouldn't be so guarded all the time.

They weren't hunters anymore. They were two members of a tribe that consisted of a bunch of shifters, Nix, and people who'd been rescued from the labs and their families. In time, even the people opposed to Orion and Perseus being here would soften toward them.

Orion knew not everyone would like him, and that was fine, even though he was a people pleaser. He didn't mind having one or two tribe members hating him on sight. That didn't mean he wasn't going to do his best to pull them to his side, though. He wasn't above bribing people with his cupcakes.

"It'll look even better once we paint and fix it," Perseus said, glancing around. "Can you imagine how nice it will be when it's full of customers?"

Orion rubbed the back of his neck. "I don't know if we're ever going to be full. I mean, I don't have experience. Maybe my cupcakes will be disgusting." Like the time he'd forgotten the baking powder.

Perseus stepped away from Teddy, even though Orion knew he probably wanted nothing more than to drag his mate home and ensure there wasn't even a scratch on him. Perseus always reacted like that when Teddy went out on raids, which was one of the reasons Teddy had asked Moore to allow him to stay home more often than not. Moore had agreed, and he tried to work around Teddy's request, but he couldn't do so every time.

Thankfully, Teddy was home now, and he was fine.

"Nothing you bake is disgusting," Perseus said as he grabbed Orion's shoulder. "There will be people who don't like what you bake and who will have all kinds of things to say about it. Most of those things won't be nice. You need to be ready to face that, but you also need to remember that other people will love what you do."

Teddy snorted. "People won't dare say anything bad

because they know you'll glare at them hard enough to set them on fire if they do. Face it—you're a helicopter parent."

"I am not."

Teddy snickered. "You are a bit, but I think Orion enjoys it."

Orion did. There were two things he'd dreamed of when he was a hunter. One of them was to one day be able to open a bakery, and the other was for his brother to be safe and happy. Perseus had always been there for him, and he always would be, just like Orion would always be there for him.

"We'll all help," Teddy promised.

Orion's heart felt like it was about to explode. "You don't have to."

"But we want to. You're one of us now."

Orion knew that Teddy really believed what he was saying, but he still felt a bit like an outsider because, technically, he was. He might be part of the tribe, but he hadn't found a mate here. He didn't know everyone who lived in the village, so there was a chance that he would, but what would be the odds?

Perseus had kept himself isolated from the people who lived in the village, but he and Teddy were together, so he'd been pulled in no matter how little he wanted it. Thankfully, Orion wasn't as grumpy as his brother, and he hoped that would help. He was a bit worried about Perseus wanting to work at the bakery because he wasn't sure most people would enjoy his scowl as he stood behind the counter, but they'd deal with that when the time came. First, they'd have to fix the bakery. Orion needed to start making lists about the things he needed to buy and what he was planning to bake.

"When do you plan to open?" Teddy asked, looking around.

"I don't know. I want to finish cleaning up first, then I'll think about it."

"I think you should give yourself a goal. We can start making flyers or something so that people know the bakery is about to reopen."

"Actually, I was thinking about opening and hoping for the best."

Teddy looked horrified. "Why would you do that?"

"Because I don't want to be disappointed."

Perseus clicked his tongue and wrapped an arm around Orion's back. Orion suspected he'd aimed for his shoulders, but he was shorter, so he couldn't reach that high. Normally, Orion would have teased him over it, but he felt like his heart was a bit bruised. He wanted to hope he'd find a home here, and part of him was cautioning him.

What if Perseus forgot all about him now that he and Teddy were together? What if Rikar decided that Orion wasn't worth the trouble and decided to kick him out? What if their father found them and attacked the village?

So many things could go wrong, and thinking about them was enough to petrify Orion. He couldn't move, could barely breathe, and could feel the panic swamping him.

But then Perseus turned around and hugged him, and everything was better. No matter what happened, Perseus would never abandon Orion. He hadn't when they'd been hunters, when they'd been forced to hurt people, or when Orion had been wounded and needed help. He wasn't going to start now, even though he had Teddy.

Orion was sure of that. If there was one thing he knew he could count on, it was his brother being by his side through whatever happened next.

"I'm going to call some friends," Teddy said as he took out his phone. "They'll want to help. That way, you won't have to wait too long to open the bakery. You should probably focus on buying ingredients, maybe start baking."

"We need to paint first."

Teddy winked. "Don't worry about that. We'll take care of it. You focus on the part you love the most."

Which was baking.

Orion leaned closer to Perseus. "You were damn lucky when you found him," he murmured.

Perseus grunted. "I'm aware. I didn't choose him, but I couldn't have had a better mate. I don't know what Fate was thinking, but I'm grateful. Maybe she was drunk that day."

Orion laughed and hugged his brother back. "Or maybe after everything we've been through, we both deserve to be happy."

Perseus looked up at Orion. "Are you? Happy, I mean."

"Happier than I've ever been. I guess that wasn't hard to beat, considering everything, and there's more that I want, but yeah. I feel great."

"You'll find someone," Perseus assured Orion, reading him like he was a book that Perseus knew by heart.

"I want to, but it's not my priority right now. The bakery is."

"The next few weeks aren't going to be easy, but by the end of it, you'll have your dream."

That was all Orion had ever wanted — for him and his brother to be safe, a place to call home, and never having to see his father again. All in all, he felt he was getting there.

CHAPTER TWO

Moore was planning another raid. Davey had been avoiding him, even though he knew he needed to try to convince him to allow him to go, but he was sure about the raid. He'd known Moore for a while, and whenever he decided it was time for a new raid, he started talking to people. He and Rikar had been having meetings over the past few days, which meant it wouldn't be long before Moore took the mutants and headed out.

Davey needed to be on that raid. He needed to ensure that Evan wasn't in one of those cages, and the only way to do that was to be present when the mutants entered the lab. Davey could ask someone to check for him, but he didn't dare.

No one knew about Evan, and for now, he wasn't planning to change that. Evan was his best friend, the man he'd had to leave behind, and he should be the one to rescue him.

That was going to be complicated if Moore didn't allow him to come along. He'd told Davey that he was being too impulsive lately, and he wasn't wrong, but Davey had to convince him that he was.

It felt like it would be easier to teach a dog to speak.

That wouldn't stop Davey from trying. Evan was out there, and Davey *would* find him.

He watched Moore through the diner's window from the other side of the street. He and Rikar were sitting at a table, both of them sipping on their drinks. Davey had spent enough time at the village to know that while Moore liked his coffee black and strong enough to melt metal, Rikar preferred herbal teas. He didn't have to ask to know what they were drinking.

He also didn't have to ask to know what they were talking about. Moore had his phone on the table, and he kept typing things, probably in his notes app. He and Rikar were having a serious conversation. It had to be about the raid, and Davey wished he could go in there and listen to what they were saying. The problem was that Moore would see him right away and stop talking, which wouldn't be useful.

Davey rubbed a hand over his face. He hated that he'd reduced himself to spying on Moore from the other side of the street. It was ridiculous, but at the same time, it felt like the only thing he could do. He didn't know how Moore would react if Davey told him about Evan. Davey wanted to think that Moore would understand and allow him to come, but there was no guarantee. Moore might think that Davey should have stayed behind and helped Evan out of the lab, that he'd been selfish when he'd run on his own, and he wouldn't be wrong. That was how Davey had felt every single day since it had happened and how he would feel until Evan was back with him.

He ignored the little voice in the back of his head that always said that Evan might not be alive anymore. He had to be. Davey wouldn't consider any other option.

He spent the rest of the meeting between Moore and Rikar trying to avoid thinking about Evan and what might have happened to him. He kept his focus on the two men, jumping as soon as they got up from their seats. They might leave together, which wasn't what Davey wanted. He needed to talk to Moore alone.

Thankfully, they separated once they stepped out of the diner. Rikar went to the right while Moore headed to the left. Davey followed him. As soon as they were far enough from the diner that Rikar wouldn't hear them, he called out for

Moore.

Moore blinked at him, visibly confused. "Hey. You're talking to me again?"

Dammit. Davey had known that avoiding Moore was childish, but he'd been angry, and he still was. He didn't feel it was fair for Moore to forbid him from going on raids, especially when he was perfectly fine. "I'm sorry," Davey apologized. "I know that what I did was wrong."

Moore shook his head. "Not wrong. Foolish and dangerous. There's a reason I ask that all of you stay in pairs when we raid labs. That way, you have someone to support you when you need it. You could have died if that bullet had hit you on the other side of your chest or even if Leon hadn't been there as quickly as he was. I know you're aware of that, Davey." Moore hesitated. "But it's like you don't care about your safety."

To be fair, Davey didn't, really. He needed to stay healthy and strong to continue raiding labs until he found Evan, but beyond that, he didn't have plans.

He never had. The only reason he'd managed to get free of the lab he'd been in was that one of the nurses had forgotten to lock his cage. He'd tried to unlock Evan's, too, but he hadn't been able to. Evan had told him to leave and that he could come back for him later, and Davey had promised he would, but by the time he did, Evan was gone. His cage was empty, and Davey had never seen him again.

He'd been looking for him ever since. Things had gotten easier after he joined Moore and the other mutants because he didn't have to worry so much about sneaking into labs on his own, but he still hadn't found Evan. He didn't care about anything but that.

But Moore couldn't understand because he didn't know about Evan. Davey had made sure of that. He hadn't told anyone about his best friend, and he wasn't planning on starting now.

"I do care about my safety, of course," Davey said. "And I'm sorry for what I did. You don't have to remind me that I was an idiot. I just thought I could help the people in those cages."

"You could, and you did, but I won't allow you to do so by sacrificing yourself."

"I promise not to do anything that stupid again."

"That's good, but you're still not coming on the next raid."

"Why not? I swear to be careful."

"I already told you that you needed to take some time off, and I won't change my mind. Try not to think about the labs and relax, all right? I'm sure you can return to work in a few weeks."

Davey gritted his teeth. A few weeks? Was he supposed to sit on his ass and possibly allow Evan to be hurt or killed just because Moore wouldn't let him come on raids for a few weeks? "You can't do this to me."

"The last time I checked, I was our leader. Everyone agreed to that, including you."

"Maybe I should have thought better of it."

Moore's expression was serious, but Davey thought he could see a hint of hurt in his eyes. It was quickly gone, though. "Maybe you should have," Moore agreed. "But it's too late. I'm the leader of the mutants, including you, and I gave you an order. You're not coming, and if you continue pushing me without actually thinking about what you did and trying to fix it, I'll forbid you from working until you get your head out of your ass."

"This isn't fair," Davey snapped.

"I don't know if it's fair or not, but I won't allow you to put yourself and others in danger. I don't know what you're look-ing for, Davey, but you won't find it by being reckless and getting yourself killed."

Davey knew he wouldn't be able to convince Moore, so he turned and stomped away without saying anything else. He should have said goodbye, at the very least, but he was angry.

Who did Moore think he was, making this decision for Davey? If Davey wanted, he could go out there and raid as many labs as he wanted on his own. That was what he'd been doing before meeting Moore and the other mutants, and he was still alive to tell the tale.

The smell of smoke distracted him from his thoughts. He frowned and looked around, hoping it wasn't a fire. He couldn't see anything, but he noticed smoke coming from an open door in an alley. There was a lot of it, and he didn't want to risk it spreading, so he ran toward it.

Moore might think that Davey wasn't good enough to go on raids and help, but he'd helped countless people since he'd escaped from the lab, and he wasn't done. If anyone needed a fire to be put out, he'd be their man.

This was a mess. Usually, Orion was decent in the kitchen, but everything had been going wrong since this morning, and it wasn't getting any better. If anything, it was getting worse.

He dropped the towel he'd set on fire into the sink. He'd set it down too close to the stove while he'd been melting some chocolate, and when the beep of the oven distracted him, the thing had caught on fire. He'd freaked out and had stared at the damn thing for way too long before finally snatching it up.

Shit. The oven.

Orion left the towel in the sink and rushed to get his cookies out. He'd been about to do that when he realized the towel was on fire, and now, thick smoke billowed out of the oven as soon as he opened it. His eyes burned, but he squinted and leaned closer to check the cookies.

Of course they were burned. They weren't quite charcoal yet, but if he'd left them in the oven a few more minutes, they would have reached that stage.

"What the fuck is happening?" a voice asked from the back door.

Orion had left it open because he'd been hot while baking, but he hadn't expected a handsome man to come running in and save the day.

The man strode in, looked around, and noticed the towel in the sink. Orion expected him to turn on the water, but instead, the fire suddenly vanished. If Orion hadn't seen it himself, he wouldn't have believed it.

The man turned to Orion. "Are you all right?"

Orion blinked and slid the cookies out of the oven. He dropped the baking sheet on top of the stove and glared at them. "I am, but they're not."

The man stared, and almost as if by magic, the cookies stopped smoking. When Orion poked at one, it felt wet.

He wrinkled his nose, because the texture wasn't his favorite, then turned to the man. "You're one of the mutants."

The man scowled. "So what if I am?"

"Nothing. I was just wondering how you did that."

The man hesitated. It was clear he expected Orion to make fun of him or maybe even do something worse just because he was a mutant. It was ridiculous, but these people didn't know Orion. They couldn't know that even though he'd been a hunter, he'd done his best never to hurt anyone.

"Water manipulation," the man eventually said. "I can manipulate the water in the air or anywhere, really. I could take all the water out of your body right now."

Orion beamed. "Would that mummify me?"

The man blinked. "People aren't usually that excited at the thought of becoming a mummy."

"It's neat. What else can you do?"

The man looked confused.

Orion didn't blame him. He'd always liked learning things, which hadn't been easy while he lived with his father. His father had always said that Orion didn't need to learn anything that didn't relate in some way to being a hunter. He thought Orion was stupid and a bit weird for wanting to know about volcanoes and space and insects as an adult.

But Orion didn't care what his father thought anymore, and he could ask as many questions as he wanted as long as this man didn't have anything against it.

Orion really hoped he didn't. He liked the way the guy looked. He might not feel attracted to him — but then, Orion had never felt attracted to anyone in his life — but the man was hot. His hair was long enough to curl, and the man had styled it so that the curls were pushed forward, covering his forehead. Some of the curls were so springy that Orion wanted to reach out and pull on them, but since this man could mummify him with barely a thought, he decided he didn't want to risk it. There was no anger in the man's green eyes, but that didn't mean he wanted Orion to invade his personal space.

"Nothing," the man said. "Is water manipulation not enough for you?"

"Oh, it's great. It's just that I know that some of the mutants are human while others are shifters, and I was wondering which one you were."

The man shrugged. "I'm just your normal wolf shifter."

"That's cool."

"Is it?"

"When you're human, it is. Sorry you had to run in and save me."

The man looked around. "What were you doing?"

"I was baking cookies. I should've waited until they were out of the oven to start melting the chocolate to put on them, but I was too impatient. I put the towel too close to the stove when the oven beeped, and it caught on fire."

"You almost set yourself on fire for cookies?"

"They're good cookies." Orion looked down at the baking sheet. "Or rather, they were supposed to be." He poked at the closest cookie again, grimacing because the texture was still weird. "You saved the day," he said, looking up at the man. "I'm Orion."

The man stared at him for a moment before nodding. "I'm Davey."

"It's a pleasure to meet you, Davey. Can I bake you a cake to thank you for saving my life?"

"I don't think I actually saved your life. I just extinguished a small fire, but you already had it under control since the towel was in the sink."

Orion rubbed the back of his neck. "Yeah, but I forgot to turn the water on."

"It could happen to anyone."

"Could it?"

Orion wasn't particularly clumsy, but he'd felt overwhelmed since he'd arrived at the village and even more so since he and his brother had been allowed out of their cells. He desperately wanted to find a place in the village, and he'd been working hard in the bakery. The sooner it opened, the sooner people would see that he didn't want to hurt anyone and that he wished to build a life here with them.

It looked like maybe he'd have to wait for a little while longer. He'd clearly been working too hard, and he was so tired that he was starting to make mistakes.

He leaned against the counter and squeezed his eyes shut. "Anyway, I'm sorry. I'd really like to do something nice for you to thank you, but you don't have to say yes if you don't want me to. I'll understand if you don't want me anywhere near an oven ever again."

Davey snickered. Orion felt a gentle touch on his shoulder

and opened his eyes to find that Davey had gotten close enough for Orion to see brown specs in his eyes. They were green at a distance, but this close, they appeared almost hazel.

"You don't have to bake me anything, but you can if you want to," Davey said.

Orion pushed away from the counter, which put him firmly in Davey's personal space. Davey's nose wrinkled, and for a moment, Orion wondered if he stank. He'd been working most of the morning, and the oven had been on the entire time. He was sweaty, even more so because of the fear that he'd set his bakery on fire.

Davey's eyes widened.

Orion got that a lot, unfortunately. When they didn't stare at him because he was a hunter, they stared because he was a big man who looked like he could hurt them. He really hoped Davey didn't think he'd do that.

"Are you all right?" he asked when Davey continued staring. "Is it smoke inhalation? Do I need to take you to the hospital?" Where *was* the closest hospital?

Davey shook his head. "I'm fine."

"You don't look fine. You're staring."

Davey took a step back, swallowing heavily. Orion followed the bob of his Adam's apple with his gaze. "I *am* fine. This has nothing to do with the smoke."

"What is it, then? If I can help you, I will. I need to find a way to thank you for what you did today."

Davey shook his head. "You don't have to thank me."

"What if I want to?"

Davey groaned and rubbed his face. "There's nothing of the kind in a relationship between mates. You don't have to thank me. I'll always help you if you need me to."

Orion blinked. "Between mates?"

"Yes."

Orion thought he understood, but it sounded too good to

be true, and he wanted to be sure. "Are you saying I'm your mate?"

Davey looked torn between wanting to be close to Orion and wanting to run out the back door. Thankfully, he stayed where he was as he nodded once. "Yes. You're my mate."

Davey had never thought he'd meet his mate by saving him from a kitchen fire. He'd also never thought that his mate would be a hunter—a reformed hunter, but a hunter anyway.

He knew who Orion was. Orion's brother Perseus was Teddy's mate, which meant Davey had seen quite a bit of him, since the two brothers had barged into their lives. He still wasn't sure what to think of Perseus, but he knew him well enough to be sure that he was nothing like his brother.

Perseus was prickly and pushed people away. Davey had only needed to spend a few hours with him to know of that. If Perseus could keep Teddy and Orion with him and ignore everyone else in the world, he'd probably do it. He was the kind of person who felt like he didn't need people in his life beyond the few he loved.

Orion was clearly the opposite. He was relaxed and happy, even though he'd almost set himself on fire. He was staring at Davey as if trying to make sense of his words, which Davey could understand since he was doing the same.

"Are you sure?" Orion asked.

Davey almost rolled his eyes, but he told himself that Orion was human. No matter how much humans knew about mates and bonds, they couldn't feel them like a shifter could. "I'm sure."

"What do you think about that?"

That wasn't the question Davey had expected, but he was already starting to see that not a lot would be like he'd expected when it came to Orion. "I'm supposed to be happy."

"I didn't ask what you were supposed to think. I asked what you *do* think about it. In your place, half of the village would already have run out the back door, and they definitely wouldn't have told me I'm their mate. You didn't hesitate, though."

It was more like he'd blurted it out without thinking. He shouldn't have, but the cat was out of the bag, and he needed to deal with what it had left behind. "I didn't mean to say that the way I did," he admitted.

Orion wrinkled his nose. On such a big man, it shouldn't be adorable, but there was something about Orion that gave off that vibe. Davey was sure that if he wanted to, Orion could do a lot of damage, but he felt like Orion wouldn't hurt a fly unless he was forced to.

Orion was tall, but if Davey had to guess, he was only a few inches taller than him. His shoulders and arms were massive, though, and for a moment, Davey couldn't look away from the muscles that bunched under Orion's t-shirt.

Orion was the definition of a gentle giant, even though he wasn't a giant. He felt like the kind of man who would pick up stray cats and fill his house with them. He'd offered to bake Davey a cake, for fuck's sake.

Davey was tempted to say yes.

"I don't see why I should hide that you're my mate from you," Davey said cautiously.

Thankfully, Orion didn't seem offended. "Plenty of people would have. You know who I am, right?"

"I do. I'm friends with Teddy, and everyone in the village has heard about you and your brother. I like your name, by the way." Davey resisted the urge to slap himself. What the fuck was he doing? If this was flirting, it was pretty bad.

But for some reason, it made Orion smile. He beamed at Davey. "Thank you. I like your name, too."

Davey snorted. "It's nothing special."

"It's special because it's your name. So you know I'm a hunter."

"I know you *were* a hunter. You're not anymore, and you and your brother are settling in. You're not going anywhere, no matter how many people don't like that."

Orion frowned. "Are there people who don't like me being here?"

Davey hated that he'd made Orion think about that. He wanted Orion to smile again, so he gently touched his mate's shoulder.

Just like he'd expected, Orion beamed at him. Davey quickly took his hand back, but it was to reach for the counter because of how shaky his legs were. If he could, he'd continue touching his mate.

"Something's wrong with you," Orion said as he caught Davey's waist and gently guided him toward a stool by the counter.

His hands on Davey's hips felt like a brand on Davey's skin. They weren't even really touching. Davey's t-shirt was in the way, so Orion wasn't touching his skin, but it felt like he was.

Davey wanted more. For a moment, he wondered what it would be like if Orion were to bend him over the counter and fuck him right here.

It didn't sound sanitary.

Orion let go once Davey was sure he wasn't going to faint or do something equally as ridiculous. Davey opened his mouth to thank him, but Orion was already gone. He flitted around the kitchen, putting things together, and Davey could only watch him.

It was a sight to behold.

Orion was big, his body rippling with muscles, and he looked like he belonged on a battlefield rather than in a bakery. He moved with ease, though, clearly knowing where everything was. As Davey watched, he put together some tea and opened a box. He fished out a few cookies and placed them on a small plate.

He was taking care of Davey.

Davey couldn't remember the last time someone had taken care of him. It had to have been Evan. They'd been taking care of each other as best as they could when they were locked in those cages. After Davey had escaped, he hadn't even gone to a healer. He'd rested just long enough to be sure he could get into the lab and to Evan, then had gone right back in.

But Evan wasn't there anymore.

Davey hadn't allowed anyone else close to him since then, and he still didn't really want to, but Orion wasn't just a guy. He was Davey's mate, and every inch of Davey's being, including his wolf, felt like their mate needed to be close.

Orion set down the cup of tea and the plate of cookies on the counter in front of Davey. "You'll probably feel better if you eat something. I guess that meeting your mate and finding out he's a hunter was a shock."

Orion was clearly hung up on the hunter thing, which was understandable. Most mutants and tribe members wouldn't have been happy to find out their mate was a hunter, but Davey was more like Teddy. Hunters were bad, but sometimes, they didn't have the choice to step away.

"I know your story," he explained as he picked up one of the cookies — thankfully not one that had been on that baking sheet. Davey was pretty sure those were ruined.

"I think everyone knows my story by now, but most people still give me a wide berth."

"Most people aren't your mate."

Orion grinned. He was gorgeous even when he wasn't smiling, but like this, with a wide grin stretching his lips, he was everything. It was almost like a child discovering something for the first time, which gave Davey pause.

Orion looked like an adult, and since he was human, it meant he probably was, but Davey wanted to check. "How old are you?" he asked before taking a bite of the first cookie.

"Twenty-three."

Davey wanted to ask more questions, but he was too busy eating the cookie. It was chocolate chip with pecan nuts, and it was delicious.

Nothing like the burned cookies on the counter.

"That's good," Davey said, even though his mouth was full.

"Why?"

"Because it means I'm not robbing the cradle."

"I know that shifters are usually much older than they look. Does that mean you're actually young?"

"Well, I guess it depends on what you mean by young. I'm thirty-nine."

Orion slowly nodded. "If we were both human, I'd wonder if it was a too big age difference."

Sixteen years was quite a lot, but Davey wasn't worried about that.

He wasn't worried about much right now beyond getting to know Orion and finding out every single detail about his mate.

Davey didn't look thirty-nine, but then, he was a shifter. There was also the fact that Orion had never been good at guessing people's ages.

Davey's age didn't matter, anyway. Orion was his mate, and that was all Orion was concerned about. He knew Perseus would be slightly wary, though. He wanted the best for Orion, and even though he knew that Orion's mate *would* be the best for him, it would take him some time to wrap his mind around. Sometimes he still saw Orion as his baby brother, even though Orion was twenty-three. Perseus had been taking care of Orion for most of their lives, and it wouldn't be easy for him to let go of that.

But Orion was ready to take care of himself. He didn't want Perseus to vanish from his life, but now that they were both safe and had a future, Orion felt it was time for him to find out what that future would be.

Apparently, it would involve a bakery and a mate.

"So we've already clarified that I don't care that you were a hunter," Davey said as he munched on another cookie. "But I don't know what you think about being my mate."

Orion blinked. "I thought it was obvious."

"Not really. Some humans don't want to be bonded to shifters, and there's the added complication that I can manipulate water. I wouldn't be surprised or offended if all of that freaked you out."

Orion was already shaking his head. "I'm not freaked out. I was actually hoping to find a mate in the village. Perseus met Teddy, and I wanted the same." Orion hesitated, but he felt he needed to be honest. "I'm confused as to why you don't have a problem with me being a hunter. I know you said that you're aware of my history, so you know I was forced into it by my father, but sometimes, I wonder if I could have done more to step away from that life."

Orion was pleased when Davey took his time answering. He wasn't throwing out the first words he thought about just because he wanted Orion to be with him. Orion understood that it was different for Davey. He felt the bond much more strongly, and it made sense that he'd want Orion to say yes to being with him.

"I suppose you could have," Davey said. "But being a hunter is all you've ever known, right?"

"Yeah. My father was a hunter when my brother and I were born. He was absent for most of our childhood, but once we became teenagers, it was clear we wouldn't have a choice. He trained us since we were around twelve."

"And, of course, there's your brother to consider. I imagine your father wouldn't have hesitated to threaten him if you didn't do what he wanted. I don't know him, but I've heard enough about him to know he's not a nice man."

"He's really not, and I hope you'll never have to meet him. He used me to force my brother to stick around. I've always been the weaker between the two of us."

Davey frowned and shook his head. "You're not weak."

"Maybe not, but it's what my father always said, and I know I shouldn't trust anything that came out of his mouth, but for years, he made me feel like I was. I wasn't strong enough to hurt people. I wasn't strong enough to kill them. I needed to do more, to be ruthless, and that just wasn't me. It still isn't."

"I'm glad you're out of that life, and I don't hold it against you. Teddy mentioned that you were hurt because you tried saving someone. That's how your brother ended up kidnapping Leon, right?"

"Yeah. Perseus and I always tried to help people if we could, but we were discovered that time. I thought I was going to die."

Davey reached for Orion's hand. Orion held his breath as Davey linked their fingers together and pressed their hands on top of the counter. Davey's hand was warm and gentle, but it still made Orion's heart race.

He might not be able to feel the bond the way Davey did, but he could still feel *something*. He felt drawn to this man, and there was nothing he wanted more than to step into his arms and allow Davey to keep the world away.

"You didn't die," Davey said softly. "You're strong, and you survived, and now, you're a member of this tribe, and you have a home. You have a job, your brother, and me."

Orion's eyes burned, but he didn't want to cry. He had nothing to cry about. His life was as perfect as he could have dreamed it. "It's going to take me some time to get used to all of that."

"You can have all the time in the world. I know we're mates, but I don't expect you to want to bond right away or for you to throw me over the counter and have your way with me."

Orion sucked in a breath. There was one more thing he needed to tell Davey. Normally, he would wait until they knew each other better, but Davey wasn't just a guy. He was Orion's mate, and Orion didn't want to feel like he was lying to him. "There's something else."

Davey squeezed Orion's hand. "Whatever it is, I'm sure we can work it out."

"I've always had problems with romantic relationships. I didn't have the opportunity to have many of them. And I refused to be with a hunter, so that made it even more complicated. But I had a few guys, and this wasn't really a problem for most of them, but I'm your mate, which means we're supposed to spend the rest of our lives together, and I don't know if that's something you'll want once I tell you."

"You make it sound like you're a serial killer or something. I'm sure it can't be that serious, Orion."

"I guess it's not. It's just that I don't have sex. Like, ever." Orion was afraid to look at Davey, but he forced himself to. Whatever was about to happen, he needed to know.

Davey was frowning, and for a moment, Orion thought he wouldn't be okay with this. He'd hoped he would be because Davey was supposed to be perfect for him, but he supposed there was a limit for everyone.

"You're telling me you're asexual, right?" Davey asked.

He wasn't running away screaming, and he was still holding Orion's hand, so Orion hoped this wasn't going as badly as he thought. "Yeah. I'm not sex-repulsed or anything, but I'd rather not have sex. I know it's an important part of the relationship between mates, though, and I don't want to ask you never to have sex again, but I'm not sure I can do it, not even with you." Orion sucked in a breath. "So if you need to take a step back, I'll understand. I don't want to force you into a relationship that's not what you want or need."

Davey squeezed Orion's hand again, and Orion could only look up at him. He was slightly relieved when Davey didn't look angry, but he still didn't know what was about to happen.

"I don't care about that," Davey said.

"How can you not? Sex is an important part of most relationships."

"And in other relationships, it doesn't matter at all. Honestly, sex is the least important part of a mate bond."

"But shifters bond while having sex." Orion was sure of that. He'd heard enough people talking about it.

"Not always. Sure, it's something that most couples do, but we're not most couples. We're us, and we'll find a way to make it work."

"I guess you could have other people."

Davey's eyes widened, and he shook his head. "There's no way I can be with anyone else, and I don't want to consider that option. Now that I've met you, you're it for me. You're the only person I'll ever want for the rest of my life."

"But I can't give you what you want."

"Can't you? What I want is love, respect, and support. I want us to be there for each other, for us to build a life together, and to make you happy. I told you, sex is the last thing I think of when I think about our relationship."

"You can't tell me you don't like sex, though." Orion knew that most people did. He didn't feel weird or wrong because he didn't, but he understood it might be something a lot of people had trouble understanding.

"Yeah, I do like sex. It's nice, and it can be intimate, but it's not the only thing that is." Davey hesitated. "You know I spent some time in a lab, right?"

Orion didn't understand where Davey was going, but he nodded.

Davey nodded back, then continued, "I managed to escape. It was several years ago, and I've been so focused on getting revenge that I haven't had time for relationships or for sex. It's just not that important to me. I've been without sex for a few years, and I can continue being without it for the rest of my life."

"But what if you need it sometimes?"

Davey raised his free hand and wiggled his fingers at Orion. "I have two hands that I can use. I'm not saying our relationship will be perfect, but I don't want you to worry about this because there's no reason for you to. I don't need sex. I need my mate, and that's you."

It sounded too good to be true, but for once, Orion allowed himself to hope that he could really have this—the bakery, his brother, and a mate.

CHAPTER THREE

Davey supposed that some people would consider him an idiot for doing the same thing again and again without getting a different result, but it didn't matter. The only thing that did was that he was stuck in the village, unable to look for Evan. He had to find a way around that before something happened to Evan, and as far as he could tell, the only thing he could do was to convince Moore to let him go on future raids.

He hadn't been allowed to go on the last one. He'd been on pins and needles the entire time the mutants were gone, then had rushed to them as soon as they returned home with the survivors. He'd looked at every single one of them, but Evan wasn't there. He hadn't been in that lab at all.

Davey hadn't been allowed anywhere near the documents Moore had found at the facility, but there'd been enough gossip that he knew they'd already found the location of another lab. Apparently, these two facilities had worked together, and Moore wanted to step in before the people at the second lab could realize something had happened.

This was Davey's chance.

This time, instead of waiting for Moore on the sidewalk and cornering him in front of the diner, Davey had decided to go to his house. It might be a bad idea, but at least if Moore wanted to yell at him, he could do so without everyone sticking their noses into it. It wouldn't be as easy for Davey to leave, but he hoped that Moore's mate would be around to keep him calm.

That hope burned to the ground when Moore opened the door after Davey knocked. Davey hated how resigned Moore appeared, even though he was right to be because Davey was here to bother him.

"Should I let you in?" Moore asked.

"I don't know. Do you *want* to let me in?"

"I'm going to be pissed, aren't I?"

"There's nothing that says that you have to be pissed. You could just say yes and let me come on the next raid."

Moore stared at Davey for a moment. Davey expected to be told to fuck off, so he was surprised when Moore nodded and stepped aside. "Come in."

"Are you sure you want me to?"

"Not really, but I'm done with this."

Davey sucked in a breath. "What do you mean?"

"Just come in. You're here, aren't you? Knowing you, you're not going anywhere until I give you what you want, but I won't consider it until you give me answers."

Dammit. Davey wasn't here to give Moore answers. He was here to convince Moore to let him go on the next raid. "There are no answers to give. I want revenge, and the only way to obtain it is to burn all of these facilities to the ground," Davey said as he stepped into the house.

It was silent, which meant that Moore was alone, which in turn meant that he'd be able to focus on Davey. He wouldn't be distracted by his mate hanging around.

That didn't bode well.

"Kitchen," Moore ordered.

He walked past Davey, and the only thing Davey could do was follow him.

He did. He walked into the kitchen right behind Moore and watched him make a beeline for the coffee pot. He poured himself a cup, then gestured at one of the cupboards, but Davey shook his head. The last thing he needed was more caffeine.

"Sit down," Moore ordered quietly.

Sometimes, when Davey was angry, he wondered who had made Moore the boss of him and the other mutants.

It had been him and the other mutants. They'd decided together that Moore would be a good leader, and they'd been right. No matter how angry Davey got, he couldn't deny that.

He just needed to find a compromise with Moore.

"You already know why I'm here," he offered.

"I do," Moore confirmed. "But I'd like to hear it from you. You know, just in case a miracle happened."

Davey snorted softly. "No miracles. I want to be allowed on the next raid."

Moore stared for a moment before pushing away from the counter. He pulled away the chair opposite Davey from the table and sat into it, still staring. He took a sip of coffee, then another, until Davey wanted to scream.

"Why are you so obsessed with this?" Moore asked. "I understand wanting revenge. We all do. I understand wanting to take down the scientists and nurses, to burn down the facilities, and to ensure that no one else gets hurt, but there's something more for you in all of this. It's like you've been looking for something."

Davey glanced down. He didn't want to lie to Moore's face.

"So you *have* been looking for something," Moore murmured. "Or someone?"

Davey knew he shouldn't look up, but he couldn't stop himself from doing just that. For a second, his gaze crossed with Moore.

"Who was it, Davey? Who did you lose in that lab?"

Davey buried his face in his hands. He'd never intended to talk about Evan with anyone, let alone Moore. What if Moore decided that what Davey had done was bad enough that he shouldn't be on their team anymore? What if he got Rikar to kick him out of the village and the tribe? Davey had only ever wanted to get Evan back, but he'd settled into this life. He hadn't changed his mind about Evan—of course he hadn't—but he wanted them to have a home when he finally found him, and they wouldn't if he got kicked out.

"You need to talk about this," Moore continued. "Now that I know something's wrong, I won't let you get away with not talking. It's weighing heavily on you, and it's pushed you into making mistakes that resulted in you being shot. I don't know what happened to you, but it's still tearing you apart, and I'd do anything to protect you from that. Talk to me. I won't tell anyone if that's what you want."

Davey sniffed. "Not even your mate?"

"Not even him. This is your secret, and I'll keep it."

Davey really didn't have a choice. He could only pray that Moore would forgive him.

"Evan and I grew up together," he said. It was the first time in decades that he talked about this, but the feelings were just as fresh as they had been back then. "We were neighbors. His family moved in when we were eight, and we went to the same school. We became fast friends, and that never ended. He's more like a brother than any of my siblings, even though I haven't seen him in so long."

Moore slowly nodded. "I understand the feeling."

"It was my fault we were taken. I was stupid, and I followed a guy at a club. I thought it would be just sex, you know? I didn't think anything of it, but Evan knew. He followed us, and he walked in on the guy throwing me into the back of a van. I've never found out who the guy was, but I suspect he was a hunter. His friends, too. Anyway, he threw me in the back of the van, and since Evan tried to stop him, he did the same to him. We were in the same lab for a while, and there was nothing I could do to help him. I had to watch as he was tortured."

Davey's tongue felt too big for his mouth. He wanted to cry, but at the same time, he felt he owed it to Evan to be strong. If he wasn't, who would rescue Evan? Who would find him and ensure he was safe?

"One day, one of the nurses forgot to lock my cage," he continued, looking down at the table. He traced a scratch in the wood with his fingertip. "I snuck out, and I tried to open Evan's cage, but I couldn't. He told me to run, that I'd come back for him, and I promised him I would."

Davey pressed his lips together. How was he supposed to explain the rest? How was he supposed to tell Moore that because of him, something had happened to his best friend?

"You didn't go back?" Moore asked gently.

"I did, but it was too late. He wasn't at the facility anymore. They'd transferred him, and I've been looking for him ever since. That's why I have to go on every raid. That's why I have to see every single survivor. One of them could be Evan."

Orion shook his hips to the rhythm of the music as he cleaned the counter. He was singing, too—badly because he couldn't sing to save his life—but he didn't care.

He was happy.

The bakery wasn't open yet, but it would be soon. Orion had been baking up a storm, trying new recipes and consolidating old ones. The front of the store had been painted, and Rikar had ordered new furniture.

Everything was going well.

If Orion was more like Perseus, he'd be waiting for the other shoe to drop. In a way, he was. With the bakery still closed, there was a chance that things could still go wrong. Maybe no one would want to buy anything from a hunter. Maybe every single recipe he tried would be awful. Hell, the bakery could burn down. It almost had the other day, and it was only thanks to Davey that it was still in one piece.

That was a bit dramatic, but still. Things felt a bit too good to be true, no matter how many times Orion told himself he could relax.

"You're going to make it rain with that caterwauling," Perseus grumbled as he walked in.

Orion grinned at him. "That's not possible."

"Are you sure? Because it's getting pretty cloudy out there."

Orion threw his sponge at Perseus's head and grinned back, and, for a moment, they stared at each other.

It did feel too good to be true, but Orion had to focus on the fact that he and Perseus were safe, and for the first time, they were free to do what they wanted with their lives.

Teddy came in behind Perseus, rolling his eyes as he walked around him. "Don't listen to your brother. You have a lovely voice," he told Orion, who snorted.

"I really don't, and you don't have to lie to me. I know my strengths, and singing isn't one of them."

"Baking is, though. Do you have any more of those pecan cookies?"

"Of course."

He turned to grab one of the containers he'd ordered for the bakery. He quickly set it up, then took out the bin of cookies and filled the takeaway box.

"What's new?" Perseus asked as he stole a cookie and stuffed it into his mouth.

Orion beamed. He hadn't yet told anyone about Davey, but he couldn't wait.

Perseus blinked, possibly because of how blinding Orion's smile was. Orion had never been good at keeping secrets, and today wasn't any different. The only reason he hadn't yet spilled the beans was that he hadn't seen his brother in a few days.

Perseus and Teddy were still very much in the honeymoon phase, so they spent a lot of time together. It felt odd not to be as close to Perseus as Orion had been once, but he didn't mind. Teddy made his brother happy, and that was all he'd ever wanted for Perseus. Besides, he'd been busy, too.

"Something happened," Perseus said, pointing his finger at Orion before stealing another cookie.

Orion put the box in front of his brother so he could reach it more easily. "Something did happen," he said, bouncing on his feet.

"Is it a good something?" Teddy asked.

"It's the best something."

"Just tell us," Perseus said.

Orion and Davey hadn't really talked about whether or not they would tell their friends about this, but Perseus wasn't just a friend, and Orion wanted him to know.

Perseus was still worried about Orion. Orion was sure of that, even though his brother was now focused on Teddy. He wanted Perseus to know there was no reason for him to be worried and that he'd be all right.

It wasn't like Orion needed a keeper, but for his entire life, he'd had one in Perseus. Perseus had kept their father away from Orion, had shielded him from as much violence as he could, and had protected him any time he needed to be protected. Even though he was only three years older, he'd taken his role as the big brother very seriously, and he still did. For most of their lives, it had just been the two of them, so it made sense that now that they could have more, they were having a hard time letting go of that. Having Teddy in his life helped Perseus, and now, Davey would do the same for Orion.

Hopefully, Perseus would feel better knowing that Orion wasn't alone and that he had someone to watch his back. It was all he'd ever wanted for both of them, and they were about to get it. Perseus already had, and while Orion still needed to talk to Davey, he was sure he did, too.

"Well?" Teddy gently pushed.

"I burned some cookies the other day," Orion explained. From the way they both frowned at him, he knew that wasn't what they expected. His smile widened. "There was a lot of smoke, mostly because I also burned a towel."

"Are you all right?" Perseus asked almost instantly.

Orion waved his worry away. "I'm perfectly fine. My white knight rode in and extinguished the fire." When both Teddy and Perseus continued staring, Orion rolled his eyes. "Davey."

Understanding dawned in Teddy's expression. "He used his water manipulation ability."

"He did. He saved the day, although not the cookies. And when the fire was gone, he realized I was his mate." Orion dropped the bomb and pressed his lips together, waiting for the reactions that would come.

Teddy smiled instantly, but Perseus appeared to be in shock. He gaped at Orion, his eyes wide as if he couldn't believe what Orion had said. To be fair, Orion couldn't, either. He still hadn't quite managed to wrap his mind around the fact that he had a mate.

Teddy stepped closer and wrapped Orion in a tight hug. "I'm so happy for you."

"Thank you," Orion said as he patted Teddy's back.

"And of course, for Davey, too. I could never have imagined the two of you would end up together, but I'm glad you did. You both deserve a lot of happiness, and the fact that you'll find it together is great."

"You have a mate?" Perseus croaked.

"*You* have a mate, so why can't I have one?"

Perseus shook his head. "That's not what I meant."

Orion pulled his brother into a hug. "I know you're worried, but I don't want you to be. I'll be fine. I found my mate, and that's a good thing."

Thankfully, Perseus hugged him back. For a moment, Orion had thought he wouldn't and that he'd demand an explanation. There wasn't much Orion could tell him. He'd found his mate, and that was that.

Perseus turned to Teddy. "Who's Davey? Have I met him?"

Orion laughed. "I'm sure you have, but if you haven't, you'll do so soon. But you don't have to worry about me. You don't have to keep protecting me."

Perseus was frowning. "I've been protecting you my entire life."

Orion hugged him again because how could he not? "I know that we had only each other for so long, and I'm grateful for everything you did for me, but it's time for you to be happy and let go. Focus on Teddy and your relationship with him. Focus on building yourself a new life. I'll do the same with Davey."

Perseus was slightly more relaxed now, but Orion knew it would take him some time to truly accept all of this. That was fine with him. He understood why it was so complicated for Perseus, and he wouldn't push him into something he wasn't ready to do.

"Davey's a good guy," Teddy reassured Perseus. "He's not going to hurt Orion."

"He better not," Perseus grumbled.

Orion looked at Teddy with a bit of desperation, but Teddy grinned at him and winked. "I'll make sure he doesn't step out of line," he promised.

"Stop making promises you can't keep," Perseus snapped.

Teddy hooked an arm around his waist and pulled him closer. "Who said I couldn't keep it? I'm going to make sure you give Orion and Davey the time and space they need to get to know each other. You'll be able to keep an eye on them from a distance, but that's it."

Perseus looked like he wanted to disagree, and Orion knew it would be an uphill battle, but it was a battle he was willing to fight because, at the end of it, he would be happy, and that was all he'd ever wanted.

"I'm happy you told me about this," Moore said.

Davey had expected Moore to berate him for abandoning his best friend, for not doing enough, and for not being the kind of person who should be on his team. He didn't understand where these words were coming from, but he was glad for them. They gave him a bit of respite, and he sorely needed that.

"I wish I hadn't been forced to," he croaked.

"I'm sorry you felt like I was forcing you, but I'm even more sorry that you felt you couldn't come to me or one of the others with this. We've all experienced loss, Davey. We all know what it was like to be in one of those labs. Why didn't you tell us?"

Davey stared at his hands on the table. He wasn't sure Moore could fully understand why he'd been freaking out so badly. He didn't understand it himself.

"I've been blaming myself for what happened to Evan since I last saw him," he explained. "I should have stayed with him. I should have found a way to get him out of that cage. I should've returned faster. I don't even know if he's dead or alive, and while part of me wants him to be alive somewhere so I can see him again, another part knows that if he is, he's in pain and hurt and that he's been tortured for years. I don't want that for him, but I don't want to lose him, either."

One of Moore's hands suddenly appeared in Davey's field of vision. He placed it on top of one of Davey's and squeezed it. Davey expected him to pull back, but he didn't. He kept his hold on Davey as he continued talking.

"What do you think would've happened if you hadn't left when you did?"

"I don't know. Maybe I could have saved him."

"Or maybe you would've been caught again and stuck back into your cage. Maybe you both would've been tortured for years. Do you think that's what Evan would have wanted for you?"

"I know it isn't, but how am I supposed to accept that? How am I supposed not to feel like I abandoned him?"

"I don't know if you can. Those are very complicated feelings, and you've been bottling them up for a long time. You've been looking for him this entire time, right?"

"That's why I always try to get into the cage room first. I need to know if he's there."

Moore didn't say anything, but Davey was pretty sure he knew what he was thinking. It had been years, so what were the odds that Evan was alive? What were the odds that when Davey walked into the next cage room, he'd find his best friend waiting for him?

He couldn't imagine what Evan's life had been like. He'd experienced some of it, but they'd been together when he did. They'd always had each other's back and supported each other as best as they could considering the circumstances, but that was before Davey left. After he had, Evan would have been completely alone. He wouldn't have had any kind of support. He wouldn't have had anyone who tried to check on his wounds and told him that everything would be okay, even though it was a lie.

He wouldn't have had Davey.

"Now that I know about this, I'm going to do everything I can to help you find Evan," Moore promised. "We can go over the documents again, and I'll keep an eye open when we raid the facilities."

"Does that mean I can continue working with you?"

Moore hesitated. Davey was sure he was going to say no, and he wouldn't be wrong. Davey's emotions were all over the place, and he'd been taking too many risks. Evan's disappearance was a hard thing to get over, so hard that he wasn't sure he ever would. He didn't think he'd ever stop looking for Evan, either, not until he knew for sure what happened to him.

"Of course you can," Moore said, surprising Davey. He let go of Davey's hand and leaned back.

He'd been convinced that Moore was done with him. He was happy to see that wasn't the case.

"But not right away," Moore continued. "You're emotional and not ready to return. I promise that I'll look for Evan myself and go through all the documents I can find. I promise that I'll leave no stone unturned to find him. But I can't risk you, and I don't think Evan would want me to. He told you to run because he loved you and he wanted you to be safe. Don't take that from him. Don't ruin your life and yourself because you feel guilty. You have nothing to feel guilty about."

Davey wasn't sure he would ever be able to believe that, but he didn't feel as heavy as he had before. Now that Moore knew, Davey found it was easier for him to breathe. He wasn't out of the woods yet, and he didn't think he would be until he knew what had happened to Evan, but it was a step forward.

They stayed silent for a while, and Davey basked in the feeling of not having to keep his secret anymore. He didn't know what would come next, but he could accept staying back as long as Moore looked for Evan. There was no one he trusted more than Moore except for Orion, and the main reason he trusted Orion so much already was that they were mates.

"What's got you smiling like that?" Moore asked, startling Davey.

He hadn't been aware that he was smiling, but it made sense that he did. "I was thinking about Orion."

Moore cocked his head. "Were you? I wouldn't have thought that thinking about a hunter would bring a smile to your lips."

"He does because he's my mate."

Moore blinked. "Is he?"

"I found out the other day. I don't care that he was a hunter. He's sweet and gentle, and I know he never would've hurt anyone if he hadn't been forced to."

"I agree, and I believe that we now know the reason why the brothers ended up here. If they hadn't, they wouldn't have met you and Teddy."

"I don't know about that, but Fate put us together, and I want to honor that. I don't care what he did in the past. I only want to focus on the future."

"Which means you have to stop doing stupid things, because you won't have a future if you don't."

"I promise I'll be careful when you allow me to return." Davey swallowed. "I feel guilty, you know? Here I am, living this great life, with a place to call home, friends, and now my mate, while Evan is in a cage somewhere, being hurt." If not worse, but that wasn't something Davey was willing or able to think about right now.

"He's your best friend. He would want you to be happy, and whatever happened to him, I'm sure he knew you're doing everything you can to get him back."

"I know all of that, but it's hard to believe sometimes."

"Maybe you should talk to Orion about this. Was he happy when you told him he was your mate?"

"He was. He's excited about the bakery, and I think he

didn't expect to meet his mate, too."

Moore chuckled. "None of us do, but our mates find us when we most need them. Maybe that's why you met Orion now."

Or maybe Orion had needed Davey. Davey wasn't sure, but he didn't think it mattered. They'd met when they had, and they would be there for each other, whatever happened.

That felt good, too. Davey had Evan, then the other mutants, but he knew that with Orion in his life, no one would ever be able to hurt him. Orion wouldn't let them. It was odd to feel so close to someone Davey barely knew, but he did, and he couldn't wait to see what would happen next. In fact, maybe he should head over to the bakery and check in on Orion.

He got to his feet. "I think it's better if I go."

"You have a lot to think about," Moore said as he followed Davey to the front door. "I'm glad you felt like you could tell me what happened with Evan, and I promise I'll do my best to find him."

"Your best might not be enough." Davey's best hadn't been.

"But it also might be. I know it's been years, but don't lose hope."

"Never."

Moore squeezed his shoulder as he opened the front door. "But at the same time, allow yourself to live. Allow yourself to be happy."

That was going to be the hard part of this.

Teddy had finally managed to drag Perseus away from the bakery and Orion. He hadn't had to try hard—it was still odd to see Perseus being so much in love with someone—but it had taken a while. Perseus was worried about Orion, no matter how many times Orion told him he didn't need to be. He might only be twenty-three, but he was an adult, and considering the way he'd grown up, he considered himself more mature than a lot of adults. He'd been trained to fight since he was barely older than ten, and he'd seen death for the first time when he was sixteen. Over the years, he'd seen even more of it and had had to kill people. He would always regret that, and he still had nightmares, but he'd learned to accept the fact that there was nothing he could do to change the past.

Orion was aware that his brother had shielded him from a lot of things over the years. They'd both been hunters, but when their father had ordered Orion to do something, Perseus usually ended up doing it for him, especially when it was violent. Their father hadn't known, because if he had, he would have taken it out on Orion and Perseus, but Orion knew how shielded he'd been, even though he was a hunter. He'd always be grateful to his brother for that, which was why he wanted Perseus to be happy and to stop worrying about him. He had a mate now, and that was who he should be focused on.

Trying to convince him of that was impossible. Perseus did what Perseus wanted, especially when it came to Orion. He was lucky that Teddy understood that and never got angry. Of course, Teddy was Perseus's mate, which was probably why he'd accepted all of this so easily.

A knock on the back door made him look up. Teddy and Perseus had already come by, and even if they hadn't, they didn't knock. They just came in and started to help. It wasn't them, but it might be Rikar, so Orion dried his hands and quickly went to open.

Davey stood just outside the door, looking nervous. It was kind of adorable, but Orion doubted that Davey wanted to hear that. Orion didn't know him well yet, but he could tell that Davey didn't think much of himself.

"Hey," he said, stepping aside to let his mate in. "I didn't expect you."

"I can leave if you're busy."

Orion grabbed Davey's wrist and pulled him inside. "I meant that I didn't bake anything for you because I didn't know you were coming."

Davey relaxed. "I don't need you to bake me anything."

"It's not a need. It's a want. I *want* to bake things for you. I want to make you smile."

Sure enough, Davey was smiling. Orion beamed at him and gently pushed him onto the stool he'd used the last time he'd come.

He looked like he belonged there, and Orion thought maybe he did. At the very least, he belonged with Orion, and Orion definitely belonged in the bakery.

Orion didn't know why Davey was here, but he decided to give him a little time. He looked slightly overwhelmed, and Orion wanted to be his rock in the storm.

He grinned at his thoughts. He was sappy, and he *loved* it.

He poured Davey a glass of milk, placed a brownie on a plate, and deposited everything in front of Davey on the counter. Davey gave him a smile that told Orion that whatever was on his mind, everything would be okay.

"I spoke to Moore," Davey said.

"Again?"

Davey grimaced. "I know. I shouldn't be pushing so hard, but I need to get back out there."

Orion didn't know how that felt. He'd never wanted to go out there and be a hunter, but that wasn't what Davey did. He saved people. He got them out of their cages and took them to a safe place to recuperate and call their families. He was a good person.

"I finally told Moore why it's so important to me," Davey continued in a soft voice. "It's about my best friend."

Orion had been cleaning the kitchen, so it wasn't a problem for him to lean against the counter and listen to what his mate had to say. Nothing would burn as he did so, and he liked that he could focus entirely on Davey.

"We were captured together," Davey said, his fingers playing with the corner of the brownie and reducing it to crumbles. "It was my fault. I was young and stupid and followed a guy out of a club. I thought we were going to make out in the back alley, but instead, he dragged me into a van. Evan followed us, so he was pulled into it, too."

Orion wanted to tell Davey that it hadn't been his fault, but he felt it was better to listen to what Davey had to say for now. Orion should let him finish his story. He didn't have all the information yet.

"We were in the same lab for a while, in cages next to each other," Davey continued. "Then, one day, my cage was left unlocked, and I managed to get out. I wanted to take Evan, too, but he told me to run and that I would return once I was safe. I promised him I would."

Davey pressed his lips together. Orion didn't know what to do because he'd never really taken care of anyone. It was usually Perseus who took care of him, and that was it.

But he felt he needed to do something. He leaned forward and pressed a kiss against Davey's forehead, smiling when Davey blinked at him. "You went back," Orion said.

It wasn't a question. He was sure Davey had.

"I did, but it was too late. His cage was empty. He wasn't anywhere in the facility, and I found out that he'd been transferred. I went to that facility, too, but he wasn't there, and I lost track of him. I have no idea what happened to him."

Davey's voice broke. Orion slid closer and wrapped an arm around his shoulders, gently pulling him closer. Davey slumped against Orion's leg and buried his face against Orion's stomach, wrapping his arms around him.

In this position, Orion couldn't hug Davey back, so he raked his fingers through Davey's curls, trying to give him what comfort he could. "You've been looking for him ever since," he said.

"Yeah. I go into as many facilities as I can and look for him in the cages, but I haven't found him." Davey sucked in a breath and pressed closer. "I don't even know if he's still alive," he said, his voice muffled against Orion's stomach.

"You can't know for sure. What does your heart tell you?"

"My heart wants my best friend to be alive so I can bring him here and introduce him to my mate. He'd be so fucking happy to know I've met you."

"He'll be happy when you tell him. I know I can't promise that everything will be all right or that he's alive, but I don't see why you shouldn't hope. You survived the labs. Countless people survived them, and while it hasn't been easy, they're still here."

"What if he's dead? What if he died blaming me for what happened to him?"

"I don't know him, but I don't think he would do that. He's your best friend. He wouldn't want you to blame yourself for what the scientists did to him. I'm sure he knew that you would come back for him. It was just bad luck that he was gone when you did."

Davey looked up. "I'll find him," he promised.

Orion nodded. "I know you will." Orion prayed that when he did, Evan would still be alive. If something had happened to him, it would be near impossible for Davey to find out.

Orion had never worked in one of the facilities, but as a hunter, he'd seen quite a bit of them. He'd talked to people who worked there, and he knew what happened in the operating rooms.

It would be a miracle if Evan had survived all this time and even more so if he was still sane. That wouldn't stop Davey, though. As long as he wasn't a hundred percent sure what happened to his best friend, he wouldn't stop fighting.

Orion would fight with him.

CHAPTER FOUR

Davey had accepted that he wouldn't be going on raids anytime soon, but that didn't mean all of this was easy. No matter how many times he told himself that Evan would want him to be happy, he couldn't ignore the little voice in the back of his head that whispered that he was an asshole for spending time with Orion and having a life while Evan was being tortured.

What was he supposed to do? He'd looked for his best friend for years. He would do anything to find him, even dying — and that was a possibility he wasn't discarding just yet.

He'd give up anything for Evan, so why did he still feel like it wasn't enough?

"You don't look like the type to be doing this job," Matthew said from the other side of the counter.

Davey glared at his fellow mutant. "And what do I look like I should be doing?"

Matthew wrinkled his nose. "Something where you don't have to deal with customers. That scowl on your face is keeping people away."

Davey pointedly looked around the bakery. There was a line by the counter and an even longer one outside the door.

Orion had opened his bakery about a week ago, and while the first day had been a little slow, that had changed quickly. Some people had come in because they were curious and wanted to gawk at the hunter baking cookies, while some had wanted to support a fellow tribe member.

Whatever the reason these people had, they'd come, and

they'd bought Orion's food as quickly as he could make it. He'd been working overtime, and even though Perseus and Teddy were already helping him, Davey had volunteered to do the same. It would be something to get him out of the house so he couldn't obsess over Evan and the next raid Moore was planning.

"Was there something you wanted?" he asked Matthew.

Matthew pointed his finger at Davey. "There. That's the problem."

"*You're* the problem," Davey snarked back. He couldn't tell if Matthew was teasing or if he was trying to be helpful. Either way, Davey had no patience for that.

Matthew gave him a sweet smile. "Can I have six chocolate chip cookies?"

Davey eyed him. There was a line behind Matthew, so he needed to be fast and couldn't afford to worry about what Matthew was up to. "What are you going to do with six cookies?"

"Eat them. What do you do with cookies?"

Davey grabbed a box and put it together. "Six cookies is a lot of sugar."

"Don't worry, grandpa. I won't eat them all at once."

"You're not that much younger than me."

"But I *am* younger than you."

Whatever Matthew was doing, it had helped, even though Davey would never admit it. He felt more relaxed, and when he turned to the woman standing behind Matthew after handing Matthew his box, he gave her a more natural smile.

"I'll see you later," Matthew called out.

"I hope not," Davey called back.

Matthew snickered, clearly showing he thought Davey was teasing.

Was he? Sometimes, he wasn't sure. He liked spending time with the other mutants, and he knew that Moore considered them all a big family, but sometimes, he wondered if that was actually the case. Sure, they'd spent time in a lab, and they'd come out of it different, but that was all they had in common. Well, that and wanting revenge on the people who worked in the labs. Was that enough to make a family, though?

Davey didn't know, and now wasn't the right time to wonder.

The rest of the afternoon was spent much the same way. People kept coming in, whispering and pointing toward the back room where Orion was baking up a storm, and Davey tried to ignore the stares while he boxed cookies and cupcakes. He wanted to be offended on Orion's behalf, but the gossip would be good for the bakery, and it wasn't like Orion knew about any of it, anyway. He was in the kitchen, where he belonged, and he'd be happy when he saw how much stuff Davey had sold.

That was all Orion wanted. He'd told Davey about his dream of opening a bakery and how his father had ridiculed him for it, and Davey was glad that Orion could have his dream without having to think about what his father would do if he found out. Orion was safe from the hunters and his father, and Davey would ensure he continued being safe.

"This all looks delicious," someone said.

Davey looked up to find Olga and her mate on the other side of the counter. For a moment, he tensed, convinced that Olga was here to tell him about his future, but she had an arm wrapped around her mate's shoulders and seemed content.

"What can I get you?" he asked as sweetly as he could.

Olga arched a brow. "You know, you don't sound like yourself."

"I don't care what I sound like. You want anything to eat, or are you here to bother me?"

"What do you think?"

Eliza sighed and gently slapped Olga's shoulder. "Be nice."

"I'm always nice," Olga said, looking completely innocent.

That was a lie. Olga was a demon. Davey would know, since he'd been friends with her for years. Eliza had only met her recently, and while the two were mates, Davey had time on his side.

"I just wanted a cupcake," Eliza said with a soft smile.

Davey couldn't help but smile back. "Of course. Which one did you want?"

"Is there any that you recommend? I'm sure you know which one is the best."

"I think they're all great."

Olga snorted. "That would be because your mate baked them."

"He did, but I would tell him if they weren't good." Davey turned his attention back to Eliza. "I really like the coconut and pineapple one."

"I'll get that one, then."

Davey eyed Olga. "Only one? I'm sure your mate would be happy to buy you more than one cupcake."

Olga rolled her eyes. "What else do you want me to buy?"

Davey grinned at her. "How about half a dozen cupcakes and maybe some cookies?"

"Whatever you want."

Davey was gleeful as he put together the order. If Olga wasn't okay with this, she would've told him to fuck off, so he wasn't too worried, and he liked selling Orion's stuff. It was good, and people should eat more of it.

"How much longer are you working?" Olga asked.

Davey checked the time. "It's about time to close. In fact, would you flip the sign at the door? I'll take care of the last customers."

Olga thankfully obeyed without arguing, and Davey handed the box over to Eliza. "There you go."

Eliza's smile was soft. "Would you want to come to dinner with us? Hansen is coming, too, and I fear he'll feel like a third wheel."

Davey playfully glared at her. "So you're only inviting me because you don't want Hansen to feel bad?"

"And because you're a nice boy."

"I'm not a boy," Davey groaned.

"To me, you all are. You're Jessup's friend."

And Eliza was Jessup's mother. Davey always teased Jessup about Olga being his stepmother now that his mother had bonded with her, but he could see how happy Eliza was, and he suspected that was all that mattered to Jessup.

"I'll go check with Orion to see if he needs anything, and I'll let you know."

Orion should have already been at home sleeping, but the bakery had just opened, so he tended to work until late during the day, even though he had to be here early in the morning. He was going to need more sleep eventually, but for now, he'd reassured Davey that he was fine and he could do this, and Davey believed him. It wasn't his place to tell Orion what he should or shouldn't do.

"Do you need anything else?" he asked as he leaned into the kitchen.

Orion was mixing something in a bowl. When he looked up, Davey smiled at the smudge of flour on his cheek. From Orion's expression, it was clear he'd lost track of time and that he had no idea how late it was.

Davey stepped into the kitchen. "It's six-thirty. The bakery's closed."

"Really?"

"Yeah. You've been working the entire day. You should probably take a break. You could come to dinner with Eliza, Olga, and Hansen. I'm going."

Orion blinked like he didn't quite understand what Davey

was talking about. Davey had already noticed that when his mate was in the kitchen, he didn't pay attention to anything but the food he was making. He was sure he'd find it infuriating over the years, but for now, it was endearing and adorable.

But then, everything about Orion was.

Orion had once again gotten lost in his work. That wasn't a surprise, since it happened pretty much every day, but it had gotten worse since the bakery had opened. He was doing everything he could to ensure it would be successful, which meant long hours of baking. He was starting to miss Davey and spending time with his brother, but he didn't want Rikar to be disappointed, which was why he was so focused.

"You don't have to come if you don't want to," Davey offered.

Right, he was talking about going to dinner with his friends. Normally, Orion would have said yes and jumped on the opportunity to spend more time with his mate, but tonight, he couldn't. "I have dough rising that I'll need to take care of in half an hour."

Davey nodded as if he understood, and maybe he did. He knew how important this was to Orion, and he'd never said anything about the time and effort Orion was putting into the bakery. He was just there for him, supporting him and helping him in any way he could.

Perseus had offered to work with the customers before the bakery had opened, but Orion had known that wouldn't be a good idea. Perseus would send them running — if they even came in after they saw his face through the window. Perseus had always been grumpy, and while his brother's offer touched Orion, he'd told him to continue looking for something he actually wanted to do rather than something he felt he needed to do. Orion wasn't against Perseus and Teddy helping him, but it wasn't a permanent solution. For now, Teddy worked in the front with Davey, while Perseus helped in the kitchen when Orion needed him to. It worked well enough.

Davey chuckled. "I can see you're still lost in your little world, so I'm going to go."

"I can come with you," Orion quickly said. "I just need more time."

Davey squeezed Orion's shoulder. "It's fine. I thought I'd offer, but I suspected you'd be too busy. I'll see you tomorrow."

Orion nodded and leaned closer. Davey pressed a kiss against Orion's jaw, then on the corner of his lips. Orion sighed in pleasure and smiled, turning more fully toward his mate so that Davey could kiss him better.

Orion didn't like sex, but he loved kissing. He could spend hours doing this, and he hoped that, eventually, he'd get to do it. The rush of the bakery wouldn't last forever, and once it was over, Orion was planning to dedicate as much time as he could to Davey.

"I'll call you when I get home," he promised.

"All right."

Davey lingered for a few moments longer before disappearing through the door. Orion sucked in a breath, staring like an idiot.

He had work to do, and the sooner he finished it, the sooner he'd go home. He loved this place, but these days, it felt like the only place he spent time in. He knew it was only temporary and that he should be glad for all of this, and he was.

On the day he'd opened the bakery, he hadn't been sure it was a good idea. He'd expected the place to stay empty, and while the first day had been a little slow — which seemed to confirm his fears — that hadn't lasted.

It was as if most people had waited to see what would happen before deciding that Orion wasn't a monster who would hack them to pieces and put them in his cupcakes. He was sure that some of the interest was because he'd been a hunter, but as long as he stayed in the kitchen, no one would try asking him questions. They'd have to get around Davey to do so, and Davey was fiercely protective of Orion.

Orion hummed as he went back to work. He liked that Davey was protective. All of his life, he'd only had Perseus, and while he didn't actually need anyone to keep him safe, it felt good to have someone care so much about him. Perseus always had, and now Davey did, too. Orion had everything he could ever have wanted. He'd make the bakery work, no matter how many hours he had to put into it.

He wasn't doing this alone. Davey had been there for Orion every step of the way, and while Orion knew that some of it was because he couldn't go on raids, he also wanted to help.

It took Orion another hour and a half to be ready to leave. He finished baking everything he'd need for the early-morning rush, put it away, and cleaned the kitchen. By the time he was done, he was ready for his bed, which probably was why it took him a few moments to realize that someone was knocking on his back door.

He dropped the sponge he'd been using to scrub the counter and dried his hands on a towel. He went to the back door, wondering who it could be. Maybe Perseus or Teddy? Orion had seen them before lunch, and Perseus had mentioned that he might return later in the day. Beyond him and Teddy, only Davey and the delivery people used the back door.

Orion opened the door cautiously because it was too late for a delivery. He frowned when he saw a man he didn't recognize standing in the back alley. "Can I help you?"

The man was hunched in on himself with his arms wrapped around his body. He was wearing a pair of sweatpants and a hoodie that was several sizes too large for him. The hood was up, hiding part of his face, but Orion could see dark blond hair that appeared dirty. The man seemed twitchy, and Orion tried to remember if he'd ever been told about any drug problems in the village.

"I'm really sorry about this," the man said, looking up at Orion.

Orion sucked in a breath when he saw the bruise that extended from the man's eye down to his chin. He opened the door wider, briefly wondering if the man was here to rob him and quickly dismissing that possibility. Even if he was, Orion could easily kick his ass.

As long as he didn't have a gun, anyway.

"Who hurt you?" Orion said as he stepped into the alley.

The man shook his head. "I didn't want to do this. He forced me."

Orion reached for the man, but he scurried away.

"Good boy," a voice drawled from behind him.

Orion froze. His eyes widened, and he looked behind the man, his heart racing when he saw his father standing there.

He hadn't changed much, but then Orion hadn't been away for long. The beer gut still hung above his father's belt, and the t-shirt he wore under his plaid shirt was dirty. His jeans had seen better days, and his hair was dirty. He looked as bad as the other man, but he wasn't bruised. He'd been the one doing the hurting, not the other way around.

Orion took a step back toward the bakery. He was taller and stronger than his father, but deep inside, he was still a little kid who was terrified of him. No matter how many times he told himself that he could kick his father's ass, just thinking it made him want to apologize and beg for his father's forgiveness.

Orion's father grabbed the man around the throat from behind. The man made a squeaking sound and scrambled to keep up, grabbing the arm that Orion's father had wrapped around him. His hood pushed back, revealing how painfully young the man looked.

"You're going to come with us," Orion's father said.

Orion was already shaking his head. "I can't leave."

"Yes, you can, and you will, because otherwise, Evan will pay the price." Orion's father squeezed the man—Evan—closer to his chest. "Won't you?"

It was clear that Evan's eyes were wide with fear and shock as he stared at Orion. Orion didn't miss the fact that he didn't say anything. He didn't even try to convince Orion to do what his father wanted. He appeared resigned, and that was what got Orion to step forward instead of running back to the bakery.

"Let him go," he ordered.

Surrounded by his friends, Davey was able to relax. The guilt still nipped at him, but it was easy to ignore when he was laughing over dinner and poking fun at Hansen.

"I can't believe you started working in a bakery," Hansen said.

"You wish you had a mate who would open a bakery."

"I wish I had a mate, period," Hansen complained. "It's not fair. Why is everyone finding their mate, but I'm not?" He turned puppy eyes to Olga. "Have you seen anything? Is my mate coming?"

Eliza was leaning against Olga's side, and Olga had her arm wrapped around her shoulders. They looked comfortable in the booth, with Hansen and Davey sitting in front of them. Seeing them like this made Davey want to call Orion and see if he was done working, but he didn't want to bother him.

The bakery was Orion's baby, and until it got a steady business, he was going to put everything into it. Davey had been aware of that from the beginning, and he was fine with it. He kind of wished it hadn't happened so soon in their relationship, but they had time. He could wait a few months, maybe even longer, until he had his mate back. In the meantime, he'd do whatever Orion needed him to do.

"You know I won't tell you," Olga said.

Hansen pouted. "But I want to find my mate. Even Davey found his, and have you seen Orion? He's gorgeous."

Davey knocked his shoulder against Hansen's. "Stop talking about my mate like that."

"I have eyes, Davey. What am I supposed to do when I see him? Look away? That would be kind of weird, and I'm pretty sure Orion would want to know what's up with me."

"You're so dramatic," Olga teased Hansen.

"I just want to finally start something, you know? I've been hunting scientists and liberating people for years now, and I've never had anything for myself. I want that to change."

"You could date," Davey offered.

Hansen was already shaking his head. "Only my mate."

Davey wished he could promise that Hansen would find his mate, but how could he? There were no guarantees when it came to mates. You met them when you least expected it, and Hansen would have to resign himself to that.

Eliza gently continued teasing Hansen, but Davey leaned toward Olga. "I'm not going to ask about my mate, obviously, but I was wondering if you'd seen anything about me," he said in a whisper.

Olga tapped her fingertips onto the table. "What if I did?"

"I honestly don't know if I want to find out what you saw. I guess I'm just asking if everything will be all right." That was all he needed to know. Honestly, the thought of knowing his future kind of creeped him out. No one should have that kind of information, not even Olga. She'd always been cagey about it, and the more Davey thought about it, the more he understood.

"He'll be fine," Olga promised. "Eventually."

Davey groaned. "That's even worse than not knowing anything. Dammit, Olga."

She laughed and squeezed Eliza closer, pressing a kiss against her temple. "Now that my work here is done, I'm taking Eliza home. Have a good rest of the night, boys."

Davey watched them leave. He wondered if Orion would still be awake and if he should go to the house Orion shared with Perseus and Teddy when Hansen knocked their shoulders together.

"What's up?" Davey asked.

"I should be the one asking you that. I've noticed you were a bit too quiet tonight. I mean, you're always quiet, but since you found your mate, I thought you'd be happier. What's going on in that head of yours?"

And just like that, Davey was thrown back to his guilt and his best friend. "I'm fine."

"That's what people who *aren't* fine say."

Davey glared. "I really am."

"I'm not sure about that. Do you want to talk about it?"

Normally, Davey's first instinct would be to say no. He'd never talked about Evan to anyone before.

But he'd told Moore about his best friend, then Orion. They knew about Evan and what had happened to him, which meant that if something happened to Davey, Evan wouldn't be left alone.

Davey was surprised he hadn't thought of that sooner. He'd been focused on rescuing Evan, but what would happen to Evan if Davey was out of commission? Who would free him and take care of him?

He eyed Hansen. Davey wouldn't say they were best friends, but they were close. He suspected that, eventually, everyone would find out about Evan, anyway, so he supposed he might as well explain the situation.

He looked down at the table as he did so. "My best friend and I were captured together. I managed to escape after a while, but I couldn't open his cage. He told me to go, and I did. When I came back to free him, I found out that he'd been transferred. I've been looking for him for years, but I have no idea where he is or even if he's alive. I feel guilty about that because here I am, living the best life, having found my mate, and Evan is going through who knows what. I shouldn't be happy when he's being tortured."

"Have you told anyone else about this?"

"Moore and Orion."

Hansen arched a brow. "And what did they say?"

Davey glared at him. "You already know what they said. You don't have to ask."

"Well, if you believed them, you wouldn't be feeling guilty. If Evan was your best friend, he wouldn't want you to be unhappy."

"But I'm supposed to focus on getting him back, not on building a life with my mate."

"Let me ask you this." Hansen tucked his leg under him and turned so he could face Davey. "How would you feel if your roles were reversed? If you'd been left behind while Evan was free? What would you do if, when he found you, he told you he'd met his mate and had built a life with them? Would you think he'd been wasting time instead of trying to find you, or would you be happy that he had support?"

Davey didn't have to think. "I'd be happy for him." He sighed. "I know he'd be happy for me. It's not like I can look for him twenty-four-seven. He'd understand that."

"There you go. I realize it's much harder to actually deal with this, but as long as Evan wasn't an asshole, he wouldn't want you to slowly kill yourself to find him. He certainly wouldn't want you to ignore your mate."

"I'm not."

"I know. I'm sure Evan would be happy for you, and it's not like you're going to stop trying to find him. You've been through a lot. We all have, and we're still dealing with all the consequences. Don't make yourself unhappy just because you feel like you have to be. There's no doubt what Evan's gone through is horrible, but it doesn't make what *you* went through any less awful."

Instinctively, Davey pulled Hansen into his arms, grinning when Hansen squeaked. "Thank you."

"Just don't hug me to death," Hansen said, hugging Davey back.

He sounded amused, so Davey wasn't worried.

Davey knew it would take him time to accept that he was doing nothing wrong, but he felt lighter as he left the diner. He tried calling Orion, wondering if they could see each other tonight, but Orion didn't answer. And when Davey walked in front of the bakery, he noticed the lights were still on inside. That probably meant that Orion was still baking, and Davey didn't want to bother him, so he didn't stop.

He'd see Orion tomorrow. He'd have to force him to take a lunch break, but he was positive he could do it. Orion seemed to find it impossible to tell him no, and Davey wasn't above taking advantage of that, especially if it was to help his mate. If it wasn't for him and Perseus, Orion would work himself into the ground. He wasn't sleeping enough, and Davey had noticed he tended to skip meals because he was so focused on his work.

There would be no more of that. Davey had kept himself slightly distant from Orion because he'd felt guilty, and even though he still felt that way and suspected he would for a long time, he was done allowing that emotion to dictate his actions. Orion was his mate, and he needed him.

Davey would be there for him every step of the way.

Orion hadn't actually expected his father to let go of Evan. There was a reason his father had brought the man here, and Orion could take a good guess at what that reason was.

He'd wanted to use Evan to get to Orion.

He knew that Orion's heart was soft and that he'd do anything to save Evan, even though he didn't know him. He would have anyway, but with a name like his, Orion couldn't help but think about Davey's best friend. He wanted to help Evan because of that, too.

Besides, the man was clearly terrified and in pain. He stumbled back when Orion's father pulled, wincing as his foot hit the ground. Orion kept an eye on him as his father dragged Evan back to the van. Orion hadn't noticed before, but he could now see that Evan was limping.

What had Orion's father done to the poor man? How long had he had him? Where had Evan come from, and who was he?

Those were all questions Orion was dying to ask, but now wasn't the time. Maybe if they both made it out of this alive, he and Evan could have a chat.

"You're going to come with us," Orion's father ordered.

"Why should I come with you?"

"Because without me, you don't have anything. Come on. Get into the van."

Orion crossed his arms over his chest and shook his head. "I'm not getting into that van, and I'm not going anywhere with you. Where the fuck were you when I was wounded and almost died? Perseus took care of me, just like he always does." Orion needed to waste time.

"How did you get wounded? Were you helping one of these animals?" Orion's father gave Evan a good shake. "You know the rules. If you're wounded, you take care of yourself, or you die."

There were no hospitals for the hunters. There weren't doctors, nurses, or anyone who understood anything about anatomy and medicine. When a hunter was wounded, they were left alone to take care of themselves. If they died, they were weak. If they lived, they rejoined the ranks and were seen as strong and convinced of their ideology.

Orion had never understood that. Didn't other hunters have family? He only had his father and his brother, but while his father wouldn't raise a finger to help him, Perseus would die trying. He wouldn't have allowed Orion to patch himself up on his own, even if Orion had been able to do it.

Orion's father reached the van and opened the door with one hand. He pushed Evan inside with the other and turned to Orion.

Orion didn't know what would happen if he climbed into the van, but it wouldn't be good. Orion had no way of knowing why his father was here or how he'd found him, but everything was screaming at him not to go. It would be easy for Orion to turn and run back into the bakery or even to the main street.

But if Orion did that, Evan would probably die.

Orion couldn't allow an innocent person to pay for something he did. He was putting himself in danger by going with his father, but he might also be able to save both himself and Evan, which was his main goal.

"Get in the van," his father ordered.

Orion glanced back at the open bakery door. Unfortunately, he'd left his phone inside. He couldn't text to tell Perseus or Davey what was happening. By the time one of them realized he was gone, it might already be too late.

"Now!" his father barked, making him jump.

Orion couldn't continue wasting time. It would anger his father, which right now was the last thing he needed. An angry hunter was a dangerous hunter, even when he hadn't trained in years. Orion's father had experience, but more than that, he was vicious.

Orion raised his hands and slowly moved toward the van. He'd hoped someone would walk by, but it was getting late, and the village was silent around them.

"Move your ass," his father demanded.

Orion couldn't waste any more time. He climbed into the back of the van, not surprised to see that Evan had curled himself into a tight ball behind the passenger seat. Evan looked up, his eyes widening when he saw that Orion was following him into the van. He started shaking his head, then stopped when Orion's father stepped into his field of vision.

"You two be good in here," Orion's father drawled before slamming the door shut.

Evan scrambled to get away from the passenger seat, probably because he didn't want to be anywhere near Orion's father. That put him closer to Orion, though, and it was clear he was afraid of him.

Orion sat down as close to the back door as he could. He couldn't make himself look harmless because of how big he was, but maybe if he kept enough distance between him and Evan, Evan wouldn't be so scared.

"Is he the one who gave you that bruise?" he asked softly.

Evan licked his lips and nodded. He hadn't said anything except for his initial apology, and Orion didn't want him to think that whatever would happen was his fault.

He nodded. "My father is going to hurt me. I don't want you to think it's your fault. It doesn't matter that he used you to get me out of the bakery. You have nothing to do with this, and it's all on his shoulders, all right?"

Evan hesitated before nodding again. The man looked like he'd been through hell, and Orion wished there was more he could do for him. He was pretty sure that Evan would freak out if he went anywhere near him, though.

His father finally climbed into the driver's seat. Evan plastered his back against the side of the van. Orion couldn't see his expression in the darkness, but he had to be terrified. Orion was, and he had at least an idea of what was about to happen. Evan wouldn't know.

"We're going to make a few stops," Orion's father said as he started driving. "You two are going to be good and not get anyone's attention because if you do, I'll kill both of you and come back for Perseus. Got it, Orion?"

Orion gritted his teeth. His father hurting Perseus was his worst fear, which was one of the reasons he was here. He wanted to save Evan, of course, but he also wanted his father to stay as far away from Perseus as possible. Hopefully, he and Evan would manage to talk a bit while his father was otherwise occupied.

Orion tried not to think too much about what his father was planning. He'd thought his father would be happy to have him out of his way, but of course, he'd also lost control over Perseus, who'd always been a good hunter. He'd also been better at hiding how much he hated their father, so maybe their father thought he could get him back in some way. If that was the case, Orion would laugh in his face.

Their father didn't know that Perseus was bonded and that Orion had met his mate. He probably didn't realize that a bunch of people would come after them and wouldn't hesitate to kick his ass if he tried to stop them. Orion didn't know how long it would take for someone to realize he was gone, but he was sure that Perseus would when he noticed Orion hadn't come home. He might be distracted by Teddy, but he always checked in with Orion before going to bed. Orion had been slightly annoyed by it, but now, he was glad that Perseus was still checking in on him.

Orion just had to resist for a few hours, and then, he and

Evan would be free. As soon as Perseus realized something had happened, he'd contact Rikar, and someone would come to get Orion and Evan. They didn't even need to know where they were. A Nix would be able to locate them.

Orion glanced at his father. He was driving and not paying attention to what was happening in the back, sure that he had everything under control. He didn't know anything about Orion's new life, and Orion wanted to keep things that way.

His new family and his mate were his secret weapon, and he couldn't wait for them to arrive.

CHAPTER FIVE

Davey spent the evening thinking about Evan. It wasn't surprising, considering he'd spoken about him more today than he had in years. Moore, Hansen, and Orion had said similar things, and Davey had realized they were right.

As long as Davey didn't give up looking for Evan, Evan would want him to be happy. He would want him to have his mate, to build a life, and to stop obsessing over finding him. That didn't mean Davey was giving up, but it did mean he might have to take a step back. He felt like if he didn't, he'd eventually do something stupid, and he'd lose everything, from Evan to Orion.

That wasn't something he wanted to happen, and while before, he hadn't felt he had anything to live for except his search for Evan, he did now. He had Orion, and even though there was some distance between them, soon enough, there wouldn't be. They'd get to know each other, things would settle down with the bakery, and Davey would stop taking stupid risks when he went on raids.

If he was ever allowed to go on one again.

Moore had done the right thing by forbidding him to continue going on raids. Davey had been angry, and part of him still was. He couldn't deny it anymore. He didn't care about hurting himself much, but eventually, he would have gotten someone else hurt, and that wasn't something he could or wanted to live with. His friends had already lost enough. They all had. They didn't need to lose even more because Davey was impulsive and never stopped to think before he acted.

A knock on his door made him frown. He'd been watching TV on his couch, still amazed that he had a home where he felt safe, but he'd been falling asleep. He'd hoped Orion would come by, but he hadn't actually expected him to. Orion had still been at work earlier, and he had to be exhausted. He was probably in bed, resting so he'd be ready tomorrow morning—which would come way too soon for him since he always got up early to go to the bakery. He wouldn't be able to withstand this kind of rhythm forever, but Davey wouldn't let him, even if he tried.

The only person Davey had protected in his life was Evan, and he hadn't done a good job. He could only hope he'd be better at it when it came to Orion. He might not have to protect Orion from scientists or hunters, but he could protect him from himself.

He hauled himself to his feet, wondering when he'd started feeling like an eighty-year-old man, and went to open. Davey would be surprised if it were Orion, but at the same time, he hoped it was. He couldn't think of anyone else who would knock on his door this late at night. Maybe Orion couldn't sleep.

It wasn't Orion. Perseus stood on the doorstep, and as soon as Davey opened the door, he looked around him as if searching for something. Davey frowned and stepped aside. He didn't know Perseus that well, but Perseus was Teddy's mate and Orion's brother, which meant they were in each other's lives to stay.

"What's going on?" he asked.

Perseus stopped by the stairs and turned to Davey. "Is my brother here?"

"No. Why would you think he is?" Davey didn't like where this conversation was going, but they needed to have it.

"He never came home tonight."

For a moment, Davey and Perseus stared at each other. Worry was etched in Perseus's expression, and it was getting to Davey.

Davey rubbed his face, knowing he'd need to feel a little more awake for what was coming. "What do you mean?"

"Exactly what I said. I always check the house and my brother before I go to bed. Usually, he's snoring in his bed, but not tonight, and the bed hadn't been slept in. If I have to guess, I don't think he returned home at all today. I thought he'd be with you and that he forgot to let me know."

Davey was already shaking his head. "He's not here. I haven't seen him since I closed the bakery earlier tonight."

"And you don't know where he is?"

"When I walked past the bakery after I had dinner with friends, I saw that the lights were still on."

"But it's too late for him to still be working."

It was, but the only other alternative was that something had happened to him, which wasn't something Davey was willing to consider.

He grabbed his jacket from the hook by the door. "Let's go to the bakery. I'm sure he lost track of time, or maybe he fell asleep on the counter. Considering how hard he's been working, I wouldn't be surprised."

Perseus nodded, but Davey could see he was still anxious. He was, too. He felt like he was about to jump out of his skin, and that would only get worse if he didn't find Orion.

He didn't even go back to turn off the TV, instead, doing so on the app on his phone. He followed Perseus down the street after locking his door, his body tense as he looked around. He didn't expect Orion to pop up from behind a flower bush, but at this point, anything would be better than not knowing what they were about to walk in on.

He and Perseus looked at each other. They didn't stop at the bakery's front door because that wasn't where Orion was.

They went to the back alley instead, and Davey knew something was wrong as soon as he saw that the back door was open.

Davey rushed forward, forgetting all of his training. He could only focus on the possibility that Orion might be inside, hurt — or worse — and he needed to get to him.

He was almost through the door when Perseus grabbed his arm and pulled him back. Davey turned, angry, but Perseus's expression snapped him out of it.

"We don't know what's inside," Perseus murmured. "My brother would never forgive me if I let you go in like this. We have to be careful."

Davey swallowed and nodded. Perseus was right. They needed to forget their emotions and go about this the right way. They had to keep calm.

Even though it didn't feel possible.

Davey was tired and yearned for his mate. His wolf was desperate to claw his way out of Davey's body and find Orion, and Davey had to reassure it that soon he'd be allowed out. For now, he needed to be in his human form.

Perseus went first, stepping through the back door and looking around. Neither of them had weapons because they weren't supposed to need weapons in the village, and Davey prayed they weren't about to walk in on anyone except Orion. It wouldn't be like him to fall asleep and leave the door open, though.

Deep inside, Davey knew something had happened. He might not want to believe it, but he couldn't deny it.

They moved carefully and slowly, checking every corner of the place before moving on. Davey held his breath as they stepped into the kitchen, but Orion was nowhere to be seen. There was a sponge on the counter, and Orion's phone was there, too, but there were no signs of Davey's mate.

"He's not here," Perseus muttered.

"Let me check," Davey said as he took off his jacket.

Perseus's eyes widened, and he quickly looked away. Davey didn't have the time to ensure that this was okay with him or that he wasn't freaking out. Frankly, he didn't care if Perseus was freaking out. He needed to find out what had happened to Orion, and he wouldn't be able to do that in his human form.

Luckily for him, that wasn't the only form he had. He finished stripping and quickly shifted into his wolf. Like this, he had a better grasp on scent trails, and considering how much time Orion spent in the bakery, it was easy for Davey to catch his.

He sniffed around for a moment, then moved toward the back door from which he and Perseus had come in. It was where Orion's scent led.

They stepped outside, with Perseus right behind Davey. He was carrying Davey's clothes, for which Davey was grateful. He hadn't remembered to mention it, but Perseus knew Davey would need them eventually.

For a moment, Davey didn't know how to make sense of what he could smell in the air. Orion's trail was there, fading but still strong. There was another trail that smelled a bit like Perseus and Orion, but not quite. It was more bitter and smelled of burned plastic.

And beyond that was a third scent trail. It smelled familiar, but that sensation didn't make sense, so for now, Davey dismissed it and focused on Orion's scent.

He followed it down the alley until it abruptly disappeared. The scent of gas was strong, so Davey thought Orion had climbed into a car.

Davey wanted to howl in anger. Instead, he shifted. "We need to get Moore," he said as he took his clothes from Perseus. "I can't be sure of what happened, but I think your father was here."

Orion had no idea where his father was. He'd parked the van behind a closed grocery store about ten minutes ago, had glared back at Orion and Evan, and had vanished. He hadn't told Orion where he was going or how long it would take him, but Orion hadn't expected him to.

The air in the van was tense. Evan was curled onto himself, his back pressed against the side of the van. He'd been silent since they'd climbed in. He never looked toward the driver's seat. His focus was entirely on his knees, but he jumped a little every time Orion shifted this way and that because he was uncomfortable sitting on the van floor.

Finally, Orion had enough. He knew that nothing he could say would get Evan to trust him, but he had to try. "What happened to your leg?"

Evan turned wide brown eyes toward him. "I'm fine."

"I don't think you are. There's a bruise on your face, and I noticed you were limping."

"I'll *be* fine."

Orion supposed he would be unless his father decided to do something stupid. He still hadn't told Orion why he'd grabbed him. Orion knew it wasn't because he loved him, which meant he had to want something from him. What that something was, Orion had no idea. He doubted that even if he could, he'd be able to give his father what he was here for. Whatever it was, his father would take it, and that was that.

Orion wanted to help Evan, but he didn't know how to get him to trust him enough to do that. After all, Orion was his father's son. Evan probably thought he was like him.

Once, Orion had been. He still hated that part of his life, but he was planning on doing everything he could to live a better life from now on. He had a second chance, which wasn't something most people got. He wouldn't waste it.

"I was a hunter once," he said.

Evan blinked at him and inched away. That probably wasn't the right thing to say to a man who might have been captured by a hunter.

"I'm not anymore," Orion quickly reassured him. "I never wanted to be one in the first place, but I was born into it. You know what hunters are, right?"

Evan gave a bitter laugh. "How do you think I got here?"

"I'm really sorry. My father forced me to become a hunter, and I didn't feel I had a way out. For a long time, I didn't. I was a kid, and I would have died out there on my own."

"So you hurt people."

"I did. I also tried to help as many of them as I could. I got hurt in the process, which is how I ended up with the tribe."

Evan blinked. "The tribe?"

"They're a bunch of supernatural people who help guys like you who were captured and hurt. Mostly, they raid the labs and help the survivors."

"I was in a lab once." Evan licked his lips. "I was there for a long time. They moved me around, but the facilities were all the same. They hurt me every time."

"If I'd met you sooner, I would have helped you get away."

"To your tribe?"

It was clear Evan didn't believe Orion, and Orion didn't blame him. He'd admitted he was a hunter, so why would he have a tribe? Why would the supernatural beings Orion had hurt so badly welcome him into their family?

"Yeah. I know it sounds weird, but the village became home after they helped me and my brother. My brother found his mate there."

"And that was all it took? They didn't care that you were hunters?"

Orion wiggled his butt a little to try to get more comfortable, but he'd lost all sensation in the muscles by now. "Oh, it hasn't been easy, and I don't expect it to be in the future. Most tribe members don't trust us, and I don't blame them. Some do, though. Some believed us when we explained that we were forced into it. I know you think it's an excuse, and it probably is a bit, but when you're fourteen and your father tells you that you have to kill someone because it's your duty and that the people we're fighting are monsters, you do what you're told."

Evan was silent for a moment. "You're not fourteen," he pointed out.

"I'm definitely not. I used to do everything my father told me because I was terrified of him and what would happen if I didn't, but as I grew up, I tried to help more people than I hurt. Sometimes, I didn't have a choice, but when I did, I always chose to help people. I still do."

He hesitated. Evan was a common name, and considering how long Davey had been looking for his best friend, what were the odds that the man was with Orion right now? But from the way Evan spoke, it was clear he'd spent years in the labs, being moved around and hurt every time he landed in a new facility. It was a miracle he'd survived and that he was still sane. He might be a completely different Evan, but he might also be Davey's Evan, and Orion wanted to know for sure.

"You wouldn't happen to know someone named Davey, would you?" he asked.

Evan's eyes widened. "You know him?"

"Well, I don't know if it's the same guy. He's my mate."

Evan opened his mouth, then closed it. "I don't believe that."

"You don't have to. Honestly, most days, I don't believe it, either. I feel like I don't deserve a mate, you know? I probably don't, but I met Davey anyway, and I want to make the most of that. He's been looking for you."

Evan quickly blinked as if he was trying not to cry. He probably was. Orion's eyes burned, and he wasn't even that involved in that situation.

"He's all right?"

"He is. A lot of things happened to him after he escaped the lab, but he found a family and a home. He never stopped looking for you."

A tear rolled down Evan's cheek. He looked down at his feet, and Orion gave him a moment to gather his thoughts. It was clear he was overwhelmed. They were in danger. Evan probably expected to die soon, and he'd just been told that his best friend was alive and looking for him.

"He's really your mate?" Evan asked.

"I swear I'm not lying to you. He'd kick my ass if I did."

Evan stared at Orion before nodding. "Then you have to be a good person. Davey wouldn't have a bad person as his mate."

Orion rubbed the back of his neck. "I don't know if I'm a good person, but I'm certainly trying not to be a bad one. I won't deny I've done a lot of damage in the past, but I like to think I've also done a lot of good. I saved people. I put my life in danger to do so, and I'd do it again. I'd sacrifice myself for you if it meant you could get back to Davey."

Evan shook his head. "I don't want him to lose his mate."

"We haven't been together long. I'm sure he'd be hurt, but as long as you were back in his life, he'd be fine."

Evan's expression turned fierce. "No. You're not sacrificing yourself for me, and you're certainly not dying on me. We'll both get back to Davey."

Orion grinned. He was surprised at the fire in Evan, but it was good to see. There was still some fight in him, even after years of being tortured. "We will," he promised.

It looked like the fight leaked out of Evan. He suddenly appeared so tired that it was a miracle he managed to stay in a sitting position. "I don't know how we'll make it happen, though. We're kind of stuck."

"We are, but someone will come for us."

"How do you know that?"

"Because my brother will realize I never came home. He's a bit anxious, so every night, he has to say good night. He can't sleep if he doesn't. When he sees I'm not home, he'll look for me at the bakery and maybe at Davey's home. That means Davey will know something's wrong, too, and they can grab a Nix and come to us."

"I hope you're right."

Orion hoped so, too. He wasn't sure what he and Evan would do if no one came for them.

Davey wanted to grab the closest Nix and force them to shimmer him to Orion, but it would be the worst thing to do. He needed to go to Moore and Rikar, get their approval, and hopefully, their help.

Davey wasn't an idiot. He knew that a lot of people in the tribe and many of the mutants didn't trust Perseus and Orion. They'd been hunters, and even though they'd been forced into it, it didn't change their past or what they'd done. Davey didn't blame the people who didn't want anything to do with them, but he hoped Moore and Rikar would help anyway. If they didn't, well, Davey was sure that Teddy would.

He prayed they wouldn't have to go against Moore's orders, though.

He pounded on Moore's door, even though the windows were dark. He didn't care if he woke him up or interrupted his alone time with his mate. He needed Moore's help *now*.

"I should call Teddy," Perseus said as he took out his phone.

"Tell him to join us here. Don't go on your own."

Perseus glared. "Why shouldn't I? Why should Moore help us?"

"Why has he helped you until now? He's a good man, and once he knows what's happening, I'm sure he'll want to be involved."

Perseus didn't look like he believed that, but the door swung open before Davey could insist. Moore stood there, wearing only a pair of jeans and a scowl.

"What?" he snapped.

Davey didn't care that Moore sounded angry. He pushed past him and started pacing the entrance. "Orion is gone."

Moore crossed his arms over his chest. "What do you mean?"

"He didn't come home tonight," Perseus explained. "I tried to call him, but he never answered, so I decided to look for him. I went to Davey's house first, but he wasn't there, either, and when we got to the bakery, we found the lights were on and the back door open."

"I think I smelled Orion's father in the alley," Davey said. The smell had been familiar but different from both Orion's and Perseus's. Davey was glad for that because he didn't think he'd be able to stand it if his mate smelled of burned plastic.

That got Moore's attention. "Where?"

"In the alley. I'm guessing here, but from what I was able to smell, Orion stepped into the alley, and somehow, his father forced him into a car." Davey hesitated. He wasn't sure he wanted to tell Moore this last bit. He didn't want Moore to think he was delusional or imagining things. "There was a third person. I think I recognized the scent, but I can't be sure because it's been years."

"Who?"

Davey sucked in a breath. "Evan. I know it's ridiculous and that there's no way it can be true, but I know what I smelled.

But even if Evan wasn't there, we need to get to Orion."

"Our father is going to hurt him," Perseus said in an urgent tone. "We can't let him. Please. I know Orion was a hunter, but he's my brother and my only family."

"Not your only family," Davey told him.

He still wasn't quite sure what to make of Perseus, but right now, they shared the same goal — dragging Orion back home. Even if something were to happen to him, Davey and Perseus would always be brothers-in-law. The bond they shared with Orion would never vanish.

Perseus looked surprised but nodded. Both he and Davey turned to Moore, who thankfully looked like he was taking this seriously.

"I'm going upstairs to finish getting dressed," he told them. "Get in the kitchen and start coffee. I'm calling Rikar and Olga."

Davey didn't have anyone to call, so he obeyed while Perseus called Teddy. Davey was anxious and felt like they were wasting time, but he told himself that it was necessary. Moore knew what he was doing, and Davey and Perseus couldn't just barge in without support. They didn't know what they would find, and Orion would never forgive them if something happened to them.

Davey had already drunk an entire cup of coffee by the time everyone arrived. They gathered around the kitchen table, looking grim.

"Davey, Perseus, why don't you tell us what happened again?" Moore said.

Davey and Perseus glanced at each other and obeyed. They had nothing new to say, and by the time they were done talking, it felt like they were at a funeral. It was clear these people thought it was too late, but Davey wouldn't allow anything to happen to Orion. If there was any way for him to rescue him, he would.

"You're sure it was your father?" Olga asked Perseus.

"I'm not sure of anything. I'm not a shifter, so I can't sniff my father. Davey says the scent smells like me and Orion, but different. He explained it's usually a sign of family, and I have to take his word for it."

"I think it's safe to assume that Davey's right," Moore said. "If we do, it means that Orion's been with his father for a significant length of time. There's also someone else with them."

"An accomplice?" Rikar offered.

Davey's first instinct was to say no, even though he wasn't sure that he'd actually smelled Evan. Maybe he'd been looking for his best friend for so long that he'd imagined it. Maybe it was because of what had happened recently and how guilty he felt. Whatever the reason, he wouldn't allow this to sidetrack him. If he *had* smelled Evan, he would rescue both him and Orion. If it hadn't been him, Davey couldn't afford to be distracted.

"Or another victim," Olga said.

"What do you know?" Moore asked her.

"Not a lot, but I think I can confirm that the person who took Orion is a hunter. I saw a van and Orion with a blond man."

Evan was blond. That still didn't mean it was him, but between that and Evan's scent, Davey was starting to believe he'd found his best friend.

And he might have lost his mate at the same time.

He squeezed his eyes shut. He couldn't think like that. He had to keep hope, to believe that he could save Orion and Evan and that he wouldn't lose either of them. It was almost impossible, but he had to compartmentalize his feelings. He couldn't risk losing it while they were looking for Orion.

"Our main focus will be Orion's father," Moore said, looking around the table. "We'll have to keep an eye on the man with him, but Davey thought he recognized his best friend's scent, so I think we can assume he's on our side."

"It really depends on what happened to him and how much he suffered," Olga murmured.

Davey couldn't afford to think about that, either. He'd only ever wanted to protect Evan, and he couldn't think about what had happened to him after Davey had run. If he did, he'd go down the guilt spiral again, and this was the worst moment to do that.

"Let's assume he's friendly and keep an eye on him in case he attacks," Moore said. "I suppose you're all coming with us?"

Everyone nodded. The sight of Teddy holding Perseus close made Davey yearn for Orion, but he told himself that he was getting him back. He'd be home soon, and when he was, Davey would never let him out of his sight. He didn't care if he had to tie Orion to the oven in the bakery, or even better, the one in his house. Orion wasn't going anywhere without Davey from now on.

"Good," Moore said. "Assuming that Orion's father is taking him back to the hunters, we have to stop them before they get there."

"What are we waiting for, then?" Davey asked.

"We're not waiting. It's time to go and get Orion back."

Sometimes, Davey still had a hard time believing that Moore actually cared about a hunter. He suspected it was mostly because of him and the fact that Orion was his mate, but right now, he didn't care *why* Moore felt the way he did. He just cared that Moore was finally ready to move and that he was about to get his mate back.

Orion's father had returned, and they were on the move again. From where he was, Orion couldn't see much, just the road in front of them. He had no idea where they were going, but he knew that once they arrived, he and Evan would be in trouble.

Keeping an eye on his father, he slid closer to Evan. Evan tensed but didn't move away. Orion hadn't been sure that their little chat earlier had been successful, but if they both wanted to get out of here in one piece, Evan would have to trust him. Hopefully, his not moving away was a step toward that.

Orion didn't want Evan to know that he was terrified. Between the two of them, Orion was the only one who had a chance to fight his father and win. The problem was that when he was with his father, he still felt like a thirteen-year-old who'd just started learning to fight and whose father beat him up every night because he wasn't good enough. Orion was taller and more muscular, he had ten years of experience, yet the little boy was still there.

Orion shoved that fear to the back of his mind when the van finally stopped. He tried peeking outside when his father slid out of the driver's seat, but he couldn't waste time. He quickly placed himself in front of Evan, ready to defend him by any means necessary.

He got up, planted his feet, and waited.

The back door creaked as it opened. Orion swallowed, knowing he was about to face his father again. He hadn't been able to do anything when he'd been forced into the van, but his father didn't have Evan to threaten Orion with anymore. Evan was here, safely behind Orion, which meant Orion could act.

He was startled when he felt a hand press against his back, but he didn't turn. From the feeling of it, Evan had gotten up, too, and he seemed to want to face Orion's father with Orion. The guy was really fucking brave, because if Orion could, he'd run the other way. It would have been easier for Evan to curl up at the front of the van and wait until this was all over, but he was here, and Orion took courage from that.

If Evan could stand up to Orion's father, so could Orion.

Orion's father took in their positions and sneered. "I should have known this would happen. You really can't help yourself, can you?"

"What do you mean?" Orion still hoped taking his time would mean that his friends and family would get to him before he had to fight his father. He'd do it if he had to, but he'd rather not get hurt. He also didn't really want to hurt his father, but he wouldn't hesitate to do so if it proved to be necessary.

Something told him it would.

"You've always been on their side. You're too soft, always have been. I should've culled you when I noticed. I hoped you would change growing up, but I see you didn't."

The thought of his father killing him because he didn't want to hurt people took Orion's breath away. He wasn't surprised by that, but he *was* surprised that his father had admitted it. He supposed he felt he had nothing to lose.

Neither did Orion.

Orion had always been torn about standing up to his father. He'd wanted to do it, but he'd known that his father would take it out on Perseus if he dared, and Orion had never wanted his brother to get hurt. Perseus wasn't here, though. Hopefully, he was coming, but if he wasn't, he was at home, safe and sound in his mate's arms. That was all Orion needed.

"You haven't changed, either," Orion said as he moved forward.

His father blinked and quickly stepped back. For a moment, he almost looked like he was afraid of Orion. Orion didn't dare hope, but he felt better once he was out of the van and standing in front of his father. He didn't move away from the van because he wanted Evan to be safe, and he had no doubt that his father would reach for him if it meant getting control over Orion back. Orion couldn't allow that to happen.

"You're still a monster," Orion spat out. It was the first time he dared speak up and face his father, the first time he dared to tell him everything he thought about him, and it felt *good*.

Orion wanted his father to know how much he hated him. He wanted him to know that he'd made Orion's life miserable. He probably enjoyed it, but he wouldn't enjoy it when Orion beat the shit out of him.

"At least I'm not an animal," Orion's father snapped back.

"You're right. You're not. Animals don't hurt people just because they don't like them. They don't kidnap people and sell them to facilities where people will hurt them. Animals don't torture their children and threaten to kill their brother if they don't obey every order they give. Animals are so much better than you, and so are shifters."

"I'm your father!" Orion's father snarled, spit shooting out of his mouth.

"You're my sperm donor. I never had a father. Hell, Perseus was more of a father figure than you ever were. He protected me and helped me, supporting me through everything. What did you do? Forced me to hurt people. You hurt and abused me. You never cared about your children. You only ever cared about yourself and how much money you could make by kidnapping people and forcing Perseus and me to do the same." Orion shook his head. "That's over now. I won't allow you to hurt anyone else ever again."

His father snorted. "And how are you planning to stop me? You were always afraid of me." He opened his arms. "Besides, it won't be long until my friends get here. Once they do, they'll take little Evan away, and I'll be able to focus on you."

Orion's stomach sank. He'd known his father was planning something, and he wasn't surprised to find that it involved other hunters. He'd hoped it would take more time, but it sounded like he and Evan needed to get out of there as soon as possible.

Where the fuck was Davey? Where was Perseus? Why weren't they here to help Orion and get Evan to safety?

Orion tried to feel for the bond he shared with Davey, but he was human, and even though he knew it was there, he couldn't find it. He couldn't use it to let Davey know that he was freaking out.

But he *knew* Davey and Perseus were coming. He just had to waste a little more time.

"I'll fight all of them if I have to," he said, straightening his back. He pulled himself to his full height, something he usually didn't do when his father was around.

His father swallowed heavily. He knew how strong Orion was, of course, but he'd always had control over him. Maybe he was starting to realize that that control was slipping and what it would mean for him if Orion got his hands on him.

"You won't hurt me. You wouldn't dare."

Orion took a step forward. "Is that really what you think? After everything you've put me through, you don't think I want revenge?"

For now, the three of them were alone. There would be no one to help Orion's father if Orion attacked him. He could leave his father a broken puppet on the ground, and no one would be able to stop him.

Orion shook his head. He hated that he was thinking like this. He had to take care of his father and protect Evan, but that didn't mean he had to become a monster to do so. He wanted to be better than his father—for Perseus and Davey, but most of all, for himself. Orion had finally gotten out of that life, and he wouldn't allow his father to drag him back.

For the first time, Orion had something he'd never had before, something that gave him strength.

A future.

CHAPTER SIX

Davey tapped his foot and glared at the people gathered in the kitchen. They'd already decided they needed to go out there and find Orion, so why were they still sitting here, talking about what they might find when they got there and what to do about Orion's father? Davey didn't care what they did with the guy. They could kill him as far as he was concerned. The world would be a better place without the asshole in it, and he was pretty sure that both Orion and Perseus would agree with that.

"We need to go," Perseus snapped, getting everyone's attention.

Davey had been about to do that, but Perseus had beat him to it. He was as worried about Orion as Davey was, maybe even more because he knew what their father was capable of. Davey could only imagine it, and even that was enough to give him nightmares.

"I understand why you're impatient, but I won't lose any of my people to this mission."

Perseus crossed his arms over his chest and glared. "But you're ready to sacrifice Orion."

"I'm not sacrificing him. We *are* going out there to rescue him, and I'm not changing my mind about that. But I don't think Orion would want you or Davey to get hurt because we didn't think about what we'd do once we get there. We don't know what we'll walk into. Teddy can shimmer us straight to Orion, but that means shimmering us to your father, too. What if he's with a group of hunters?"

"Then Orion is in even more danger than we thought."

"Yes, but we won't be able to help him if we get caught, too. We won't be able to help him if the hunters hurt or kill us. We don't know what your father wants from Orion, but it might be a trap."

Davey swallowed and leaned harder against the counter. He hadn't even thought about that, which was probably why he'd never be the leader of the mutants. It was a good thing he didn't want to be. It was way too much responsibility, and it was clear he didn't have it in him to shoulder it.

He didn't want anyone to get hurt, but rescuing Orion was still his main goal. He'd go alone if he had to, but when he glanced at Perseus, he realized he wouldn't have to. Perseus was as focused as Davey was on getting Orion home.

"It might be one," Perseus agreed. "But that won't be enough for me to leave my brother behind."

"Again, I'm not asking you to do that. We don't leave people behind, ever."

"He's not one of you."

"He might as well be. He's Davey's mate, isn't he? Davey is one of us, and that extends to the people he loves and of course, his mate."

Davey's mouth went dry. He didn't love Orion just yet, but Orion was his mate. It was a question of time before he did.

If he got to have the time. If they got to Orion in time and rescued him before he got hurt.

Moore pushed away from the table and got to his feet. "I think we have everything hammered down," he said, still looking at Perseus. "I won't ask you to stay behind because I know what your answer would be if I did, but you need to let us handle this."

Perseus bristled. "Why should I?"

"Because this is our job."

"Protecting my brother is *my* job, and I won't let anyone

stop me from doing it, not even you." He hesitated. "I like you, Moore, and I'm grateful for the opportunity you gave me and Orion. You and Rikar welcomed us into your family and into your home, and it meant a lot for both of us, but especially for my brother. He never thought he'd have a home, and you gave him that. I'll always be grateful, but Orion comes first. If I have to disobey your orders to save him, I will. If I have to fight my father and kill him, that's what I'll do."

Moore stared at him for a moment, possibly to understand he was being serious. Davey didn't have to think about it. He knew that Perseus was. Before he'd met Teddy, Orion had been the center of Perseus's world. In a way, he still was. He was Perseus's little brother, and that meant everything to Perseus. He wasn't kidding when he said he'd sacrifice himself and everything he had to save his brother.

Teddy squeezed Perseus's shoulder, possibly to let him know he would support him. Davey wasn't surprised. Teddy was a mutant, and Moore and the rest of them were important to him, but Perseus was his mate. He'd always be on Perseus's side, just like Davey would always be on Orion's. Nothing would ever change that.

Moore sighed. "I won't try to stop you if you have to deal with your father. It's not my business, and frankly, it would probably help our cause if you did. Just don't put yourself in danger."

"You almost sound like you care."

"I do. Teddy loves you, and I love Teddy."

Teddy's cheeks went pink. "You didn't have to use those words."

Moore arched a brow at him. "Why not? You do love him. He's your mate."

"There was no need to say it in front of everyone."

Davey didn't have time to wonder what the fuck was happening, and honestly, he didn't care. "Are we going?"

Moore nodded once. "We are. And all of this goes for you, too, Davey. I know you want to save your mate, and I won't try to stop you, but you need to be careful. Orion would never forgive himself if something happened to you while you're rescuing him."

He was right, which was why Davey had no intention of doing anything stupid. This wasn't his first rodeo, though. He'd raided dozens of labs and had fought even more guards. He was trained, he could shift into a wolf, and he could use water manipulation. Whatever happened, he'd be able to face it.

"Are you willing to shimmer all of us together?" Moore asked Teddy.

"Of course." Teddy's expression was set. He was probably eager to get to Orion and shimmer him back home.

"Let's go, then, and be careful," Moore ordered.

They couldn't shimmer from inside the house, so they all filed toward the front door. Moore stayed behind for a few moments, no doubt to say goodbye to his mate. Jolyn would be waiting for him at home, worrying and wondering what was happening. Davey wasn't sure how he did it, but he was glad he wouldn't have to.

Teddy didn't go far. He was just out of range of the Nix blockers when he held out his hands for everyone to grab. Davey crowded close to Perseus, and they exchanged a glance when they both grabbed onto Teddy. Whatever happened, they were in this together. Their only goal was to bring Orion home safely.

Davey couldn't care less what happened to Orion's and Perseus's father. If the man was killed, it would be good riddance. If he wasn't, he'd get what he deserved eventually, even if it didn't come from Perseus.

"Ready?" Teddy asked.

"As ready as we'll ever be," Olga answered.

Davey kept his eyes open, even though it felt weird. He wanted to be ready to defend himself and his friends when they arrived. They had no idea what they would find when they did.

He let go of Teddy as soon as the ground felt steady under his feet. He looked around, ready to suck the water out of anyone who stood in his way. Thankfully, it didn't seem to be a trap because there were only two people standing there.

Orion was facing his father. He had his back toward a van with open doors. His father was threatening him, and Davey had to work hard to keep his wolf in because they both wanted to kick the man's ass.

"Olga, Teddy, take a look around," Moore ordered. "Make sure there are no people hiding in the bushes."

They nodded and vanished into the darkness, but Davey stayed where he was. Orion didn't seem to be in danger at the moment. He was talking back to his father, standing up to him, but even if his father snapped and tried to attack him, Orion should be able to have the upper hand. He was taller and broader. He had less experience, but brute strength would probably be enough.

And if it wasn't, Davey would step in. He could tear Orion's father apart and ensure that nothing was left of him except pieces no one would be able to put back together.

Perseus moved forward, but Moore clamped a hand on his shoulder. Davey wasn't surprised when Perseus tried to pull away, but Moore shook his head.

"We're close enough to intervene if we have to, but I think your brother needs to confront your father."

It tore Davey's heart apart to stand there without doing anything, but Moore wasn't wrong. Orion's father was a dark cloud over Orion's otherwise bright future, and it would be better if Orion could deal with him now. Maybe once he did, he would finally be free of his father and the hunters.

This wasn't a battle Davey could fight for him, unfortunately.

Orion had noticed the people who'd just arrived. He hadn't looked their way because he didn't want to be distracted, but he was sure it was Perseus and Davey.

Knowing they were there, ready to help him if he needed them to, made him feel stronger. His father had always told him that he was weak and that because of that, he should've gotten rid of him when he was young, but Orion knew that wasn't the truth. He wasn't weak. He was strong enough to admit when he needed help, to allow others to step in when he couldn't do something, and that was something his father would never understand. He didn't know what being a family meant. They might be related by blood, but they'd never been one.

Orion watched as his father glanced sideways. He paled, and Orion wondered who had made him react that way. Beyond Perseus and Davey, Orion didn't know who was there, although he could guess that Teddy had been the one to shimmer them here. Maybe seeing the three of them there, ready to help Orion, was enough to get Orion's father to freak out.

Orion didn't care. He was done with all of this. He wanted to go to his mate and tell him he'd found Evan. He wanted to reassure his brother that he was fine and that their father would never hurt either of them again.

"Where are your friends?" he asked. "How many are supposed to arrive? Will there be enough of them to beat me and my friends?"

"We won't allow you to take over the world," Orion's father snarled. "It belongs to humans, not these—these animals."

Orion grinned. "Want to know something? Turns out, I'm

a wolf shifter's mate."

Orion's father gaped for a second. Orion had always tried not to provoke his father because he hadn't wanted to deal with the consequences, but he'd seen Perseus do it time and time again. He knew what his father would do. He knew what always happened when his father got so angry that he couldn't think anymore.

Orion's father screamed and ran toward him. He probably wanted to shake some sense into Orion and make him see that being with a shifter wasn't what he was supposed to do. Maybe he'd even kill him for being a shifter's mate, but Orion wouldn't allow him to do any of that. He was done with this. He was done with bowing to his father and begging for scraps of affection he'd never get. His father was out of his life, and he'd never been happier.

Once Orion's father was close enough, he swung his arm back to punch Orion. He was still fast, even though it had been years since he'd last fought, but he wasn't as fast as Orion. He also wasn't as strong, and when the punch came toward Orion's face, Orion caught it easily. He squeezed his fingers around his father's fist, then twisted his father's arm. His father had to move with it if he didn't want Orion to break it, but he struggled to get away.

Orion kicked his father's legs from under him, and when he went down, he pressed him against the ground with his knee. His father was face down in the dirt—where he belonged.

Orion had always been terrified of the man wriggling under him, and maybe initially, he'd been right to be. When he was a child, his father had always seemed larger than life. It would have been easy for him to hurt Orion and Perseus, and he had. He'd tortured them for years, had brainwashed them, had made them think that they were nothing more than weapons and that they would never be loved.

But they *were* loved. Perseus had Teddy, and even though Orion and Davey hadn't known each other long, Orion was sure that was where they were headed.

He couldn't wait.

His father wasn't scary anymore. He was just an asshole who would die alone. He'd had a family, but he'd hurt them instead of cherishing them, and he'd lost them.

Orion didn't feel sorry for his father. He never had, and he never would.

Orion pushed his father harder into the dirt one last time before releasing him. His father stayed where he was for a moment, panting, but Orion was done. "I hope I never see you again," he murmured as he turned.

He desperately wanted to go to Davey, but he felt the need to check in on Evan first. The poor man was still in the van, his eyes wide as he stared at Orion. Orion raised his hands, hoping Evan would understand that he wasn't about to attack him. Orion hoped he'd never have to do that ever again. He didn't want to hurt people. He wanted to feed them cupcakes and make them happy.

"Are you all right?" he asked Evan.

Evan quickly nodded, but he was still staring at Orion's father.

"You think you can come out of the van?"

Evan hesitated. "I don't know. I'm scared."

"It's all right to be scared."

"You weren't."

"Oh, I was. I was terrified, Evan."

"You didn't look scared."

"I knew what my father would do. I was prepared, and besides, I had to protect you. No matter how scared I was, I couldn't listen to the fear."

Evan was still hesitant. He wasn't looking at Orion's father anymore, his gaze skittering from Orion to the area around the van instead. He had to have seen that people had arrived. Maybe that was why he was so hesitant.

"These are my friends, so you don't have to be afraid of them," Orion said soothingly. "Remember I told you they would come for me? Well, they did, and they'll help you, too."

"Really?"

Evan sounded so fucking young. Orion didn't have to ask him to know that he'd been through hell over the past years, and it was a miracle that he was still alive and had so much fight in him. Anyone else in his place would have been reduced to a puddle of fear, but not Evan. He still had the courage to reach out to take Orion's hand when Orion offered it to him.

Evan's gaze flickered to something behind Orion, and he scrambled back. Orion swiftly turned around, not surprised to see that his father hadn't stayed down. Orion had known better, but once again, he'd wanted to hope.

He shouldn't have.

And his father shouldn't have tried to attack him again. He might not know who the people who'd joined them were beyond Perseus, but he had to have known that Perseus wouldn't let him hurt Orion. Maybe he'd thought he could be fast enough before Perseus kicked his ass.

But Orion didn't just have Perseus. He had Davey, too, which was why his father was encased in what looked like a box made of water.

"Do you know how much humidity there is in the air right now?" Davey asked as he stepped toward Orion's father. "Enough to surround you with water. Enough to drown you."

Evan sucked in an audible breath behind Orion. He'd probably seen Davey.

"Is that what you want me to do?" Davey continued as he stopped in front of Orion's father. "I wouldn't regret it. I know what you did to your sons, and one of them is my mate.

I'd do anything to have you out of Orion's life, including killing you. You don't deserve to live, anyway."

"That's not for you to decide," Orion's father said. His voice trembled as if he was afraid, and maybe he was. For the first time, he'd finally encountered someone who fought back. Orion had, but his father had never thought Orion and Perseus were good enough to take him down. He'd always underestimated them.

But Davey wasn't Orion or Perseus. It was clear he wouldn't hesitate to kill, and for a moment, Orion hoped he would.

"He was going to attack you from behind," Evan murmured. He'd moved closer again, and Orion could feel the heat of his body against his back. They weren't touching, but it was a close thing.

"Good thing my mate stepped in, then," Orion murmured back.

"You weren't lying. You really are Davey's mate."

"I am, and he'll be over the moon to find you here. He's been looking for you. He never stopped."

"I never expected him to stop." Evan hesitated. "I'm just not sure what to do. It's been so long, and I feel like my life back then doesn't even belong to me. It's like it was a dream."

Orion turned to look at him. "Well, if it was a dream, you're still living it. You're free, Evan. You're free, and you have Davey back." And if he was okay with that, he'd also have Orion and the rest of their family. He was going to need all the help he could get.

Luckily for him, he wasn't alone anymore.

Davey wouldn't allow anyone to hurt Orion. It was taking everything he had not to just drown the asshole without asking Orion what he wanted, but he didn't want to risk his mate hating him because he'd killed his father. Orion's heart was soft, so Davey wouldn't be surprised if he decided it was okay to let his father go.

There was no chance of that happening. Even if Davey didn't kill the guy, Moore wouldn't let him return to the hunters. Davey doubted that Orion's father would give them any kind of information about the hunters, but that was all right. They didn't need any more information, not if it came from a man like him. They could defeat the hunters without him.

"Don't kill him," Moore cautioned Davey.

"I don't know. I'm feeling particularly bloodthirsty today."

Moore stopped in front of Orion and Perseus's father. He stared at him for a moment, and Davey noticed his eyes widening just a bit. "Mitchell. I bet you didn't think you'd ever see me again."

Davey's eyes went wide. Moore knew the guy? Orion's father said something, but Davey couldn't hear it since the asshole was surrounded by water. He'd left him a bubble of air so he wouldn't die, but he lowered the water until Mitchell's head poked out. "I should have killed you when I had the chance," Mitchell snarled.

For some reason, Moore seemed to find that hilarious. "You? You wouldn't have killed me. You weren't strong enough to do so when I was in a cage, and you're certainly not strong enough to do it now."

"What's going on?" Perseus asked. "How do you know my father?"

"You're aware that he worked in a lab before he became a hunter, right?"

Davey blinked. He hadn't expected that, but he supposed it made sense.

"Did he work in the lab you were in?" Perseus asked.

"He did. He was one of the cruelest guards. He pushed us around, never hesitated to use force if we dared resist, and when the scientists didn't need us anymore, he took great pleasure in killing us. He's a monster."

Perseus nodded. "I agree. Are you going to kill him?"

"I'm tempted. You think he'd give us information about the hunters?"

Perseus snorted. "I doubt it. But even if he did, I don't think you'd get anything interesting or useful. He might have been a good hunter before, but he's an old man now. No matter how much he boasts about being in charge, he's not."

"How dare you?" Mitchell snapped while reaching for Perseus. "I made you who you are. Without me, you would've died a long time ago."

Perseus sniffed. "In some ways, it would have been better. I have to thank you, though. You didn't kill me, which meant I lived long enough to meet my mate." Perseus smiled, showing Mitchell his teeth. "Isn't that ironic? You're a hunter who hates all supernatural beings, and both your sons found their mates."

Mitchell tried to get to Perseus, and Davey increased the pressure of the water around him. He wasn't above getting Mitchell's head back in and letting him drown. He didn't even care if Moore stared at him with his disappointed-dad expression.

"How long can you go without breathing, Dad?" Perseus asked, leaning forward. "Because I wouldn't mind watching Orion's mate kill you."

Mitchell's eyes were wide as he glanced at Davey. Davey gave a little wave, his smile widening when Mitchell looked like he wanted to kill him. He probably did.

"You see what your labs have been doing to people?" Davey asked. "They gave us extra powers. They made us even stronger and more dangerous. Your hunters will be decimated sooner rather than later, and I kind of hope that you'll be alive to see it. It's a good punishment, isn't it? You wanted to kill your sons, but in the end, you'll be the one to die."

"This is getting creepy," Moore muttered. He squeezed Davey's shoulder. "Let go of him. I'll have Teddy take him back." He turned to Teddy. "Lock him up."

"He said that more hunters were coming," Orion warned.

Davey's attention snapped back to him. He'd been so focused on wanting to keep them safe that he hadn't checked in on him yet. He'd been about to do that when he'd seen Mitchell move toward him, and he hadn't thought before reacting and stopping him. Now that he wouldn't have to keep Mitchell in his water coffin, Davey would be able to focus on his mate.

Moore nodded, and Davey let go of the water. He stayed where he was for a moment just to be sure that Mitchell wouldn't do anything stupid, but Teddy was on him in seconds. He grabbed Mitchell's arm, wrinkled his nose in what appeared to be disgust, and vanished.

Davey turned to Orion. He was hovering by a van that had no doubt been used to bring him here, almost as if he wasn't sure it was safe for him to step away. Davey rushed forward, not wanting to waste one more second. Orion beamed when he saw him and opened his arms, and Davey dove into them.

Orion wrapped himself around him, and everything was good in Davey's world again. He had Orion back, and Orion was safe. There was nothing more Davey could have asked for.

But the universe had apparently decided that after everything Davey had been through, he'd earned himself some happiness. He'd only been hugging Orion a few seconds when Orion gently pushed him away. For a moment, Davey wondered if maybe Orion had changed his mind about being with him. He'd wait for years if he needed more time. He didn't care how long.

"There's someone here for you," Orion said.

Davey frowned and cocked his head. "What do you mean? Someone other than you?"

Orion grabbed Davey's shoulders and turned him so he'd face the van. The doors were open, and a lone figure stood there, staring at Davey.

Davey's knees buckled. He grabbed Orion's arm to keep himself upright, thankful that his mate was there. Orion didn't let go of Davey. He pulled him closer and wrapped an arm around his waist, holding him up. "Evan didn't believe me when I first told him I was your mate," Orion said softly. "But he does now."

Evan made a wounded sound that Davey knew would haunt his nightmares, but he didn't care. When he stumbled forward, Evan scrambled out of the van and threw himself into his arms. The force of the impact made Davey stumble back, but once again, Orion was there. He caught both of them, wrapping his big arms around them as if shielding them from the world.

Davey had found Evan.

Well, it was more that somehow, *Orion* had found Evan, but Davey didn't care who had. He'd been looking for years, praying that Evan would still be alive but also telling himself that he needed to be prepared in case Evan wasn't. He'd never expected to find Evan out of a lab, but here he was.

Davey gently pushed Evan away and stared down at him. "How are you here?"

Evan shrugged. He clung to Davey as if he wasn't planning on letting go of him anytime soon, and while that might make things awkward, Davey was happy with it. It would be a while before he would let Evan out of his sight.

"He was supposed to take me to a new lab. I was getting transferred."

What were the odds that Orion's father, of all people, would transfer Evan? Maybe Fate really had decided that it was time for Davey to stop hurting all the time. She'd given him his mate, and now, she was giving him Evan back.

Davey had been happy in his life, even recently, but he didn't think he'd ever felt so light. His life had gone from being a disaster to this, and he wouldn't have it any other way.

He had his mate and now Evan. As far as he was concerned, that was everyone he needed.

Once Orion was sure that Davey and Evan wouldn't fall on their faces, he took a step back. He wanted to give them space to reunite, and he had his own reunion to attend.

He turned to find Perseus striding toward them. He opened his arms, and Perseus didn't hesitate to wrap himself around him and squeeze hard enough to cut off circulation in his torso.

"I still need to breathe," Orion complained.

"You can breathe once I'm done hugging you," Perseus said, but he did loosen his hold on Orion.

He didn't let go, but that was fine with Orion. He was having a hard time letting go, too.

They clung to each other for a while, and Orion prayed they'd never be separated again. He'd known Perseus and Davey would come for him, but it hadn't been easy. He hoped he'd never have to deal with his father again.

Moore cleared his throat. "I don't want to bother any of you, but Orion, you said your father mentioned more hunters?"

"Yeah. He said they were coming."

That made Moore smile, which wasn't the reaction Orion had expected. "Maybe it's time we address the hunter problem rather than focus on the labs. The two of you should go home, though. I don't want you to have to kill people you know."

Perseus rolled his eyes. "I wanted to kill all of them when I was a hunter, never mind now. We'll be fine, although Orion should go home with Davey." His gaze flickered on the van. "And whoever the man Davey is hugging the hell out of."

"That's Evan, Davey's best friend."

Moore blinked, visibly surprised. "You found Evan?"

"I didn't exactly find him. He was already with my father."

"I don't think that's how Davey will see it. If he didn't love you already, he will now."

Orion shuffled his feet. "I didn't do anything."

Moore squeezed his shoulder. "Not on purpose, but you were there for Evan."

Teddy chose that moment to reappear. Moore hurried toward him, no doubt to tell him he'd have to go back to pick up the others. If they were going to fight the hunters, they would need more fighters. Orion didn't want to be one of them, but he would be if he had to. He just wanted all of this to be over, and getting rid of the hunters would be the best way to do that.

Moore gestured at Orion and Perseus to come closer. When they did, he nodded toward Teddy. "Teddy will take both of you and Davey and Evan back to the village. More people are coming, so he can stay with you. None of you will have to return to fight."

"What if I do want to fight?" Perseus asked. "Some of these hunters made my life hell. I wouldn't mind kicking their ass."

"Even if the hunters who made your life hell arrive, I don't want you to have anything to do with them. You're not a hunter anymore, Perseus."

Perseus's shoulders slumped, but he nodded. "Fine. I'll go home with my mate."

Moore turned to Orion. "That's all right with you?"

"I can't wait to get a good night's sleep." Orion grimaced. "Or a few hours, anyway."

"Take the day off. No one will mind not having fresh doughnuts, especially after they find out about all of this. Besides, I'm sure you and Davey will want to spend some time with Evan. I'd be surprised if Davey allowed you out of his sight for the next few days."

Orion grinned. "That's good, because I don't want to be away from him."

"That shouldn't be a problem. Go get your mate."

Orion left Teddy and Perseus and moved back toward the van. Davey and Evan were still standing there, but they weren't hugging anymore. Orion didn't fail to notice that they were still touching, though. Davey had wrapped his fingers around Evan's wrist and was clinging to him as if he was afraid that if he didn't, Evan would vanish. Considering that was pretty much what had happened all those years ago, it wasn't a surprise. Orion wished his mate hadn't had to go through all of this, but in the end, everything had worked out. Davey had Evan back, and Evan was safe. His road to recovery wouldn't be easy, but it could finally start.

Orion cleared his throat, getting their attention. "We're headed home."

"What about the other hunters? You said they were coming?" Davey asked.

"They are, but Moore wants us away from the fight."

Davey nodded and pulled Evan forward. Evan followed, but he seemed hesitant, and Orion wasn't quite sure why he felt that way.

"Everything okay?" he asked. They weren't friends, but considering what they'd been through together, Orion felt close to him. The fact that Evan was his mate's best friend probably also helps.

"Where am I going to stay?" Evan asked.

"With me," Davey declared. "I have an entire house to myself, and I want you there with me."

It would take some time for the two of them to be comfort-able with being away from each other, but that was fine. Orion liked Evan, and he wanted Davey to be happy. If that meant that Evan and Davey would be roommates for the time being or even the rest of their lives, Orion was perfectly happy with that.

Evan looked from Davey to Orion. "Are you sure? I don't want to be a bother."

"I'm sure," Davey said without looking at Orion.

When Evan glanced at him again, Orion nodded. "Let's go home," he said, holding out one hand to Davey.

Davey took it, then grabbed Evan's hand and pulled him forward. It looked like, for the time being, Evan would be part of the relationship between Davey and Orion, but that was fine. Orion didn't need Davey to be entirely focused on him. Besides, he wanted to help Evan, too. There was no way to know what had happened to him over the years, but it couldn't be good, and Orion wanted to be there for him, even though he didn't know him. No one should have to go through what he went through, and if they did, they shouldn't have to heal without support. Orion would be around Evan so much that Evan would wish he wasn't.

Orion pulled Davey and Evan toward Teddy. He was talk-ing with Perseus, but both of them looked up when they got close. Orion grinned and gestured at Evan. "Guys, this is Evan, Davey's best friend. Evan, this is my brother, Perseus, and his mate, Teddy. Teddy's going to take us home."

Evan looked overwhelmed, which was understandable. Still, he managed to nod, and when Teddy held out a hand, he didn't hesitate to take it. Perseus grabbed Teddy's other hand, so Orion squeezed Teddy's shoulder and pulled Davey closer. It was a tight fit, but they wouldn't have to stand like this for long.

Sure enough, a few seconds later, they were home in the

village. Evan blinked and stepped away, but Davey didn't let go of him. Orion suspected it would be a while before Davey could do that.

"We should get a healer for Evan," he said.

Davey snapped his face toward Evan. "Why? Were you hurt?"

"I'm fine," Evan muttered.

"You should get that bruise seen, anyway. Is there anything else?"

"He's limping," Orion explained.

Evan shot him a look of betrayal, but it made Orion smile. Evan didn't seem angry, thankfully, and when Orion stepped closer, he leaned against him. It surprised Orion, considering how they'd met and the fact that Evan knew Orion had been a hunter, but maybe he trusted him.

"Why don't you head to Davey's place?" Teddy suggested. "Perseus and I will find Leon and send him your way. I could do it, but considering what I know about Evan's situation, I'd feel more comfortable if someone who knows what they're doing does this instead of me."

"That would be for the best," Davey agreed.

Orion looked down at Evan. "I can carry you home if you want. It's not far, but I'm not sure how comfortable you are walking."

Evan hesitated, then nodded quickly. He probably wasn't used to people helping him and taking care of him, but that would change soon. Evan would have to deal with Davey's protectiveness, and Orion wouldn't be far behind. He might not know Evan well, but he was already part of his family, and family meant everything to Orion. Only his brother had been part of it before, but Orion had enough love for all of his new family members.

Including Evan.

CHAPTER SEVEN

Davey was at peace, which wasn't a feeling he was used to. For so long, he'd been tortured by the fact that he'd abandoned his best friend and that Evan was being hurt, and there was nothing Davey could do to help him. He hadn't even known where Evan was or if he was dead or alive, and while he'd kept hoping all these years, part of him had been convinced it was for nothing. The odds that Evan would be alive were so tiny that it didn't actually feel possible.

But Evan *was* alive, and he was at the bakery right now. He'd always been a good baker, but it had been years since he'd last been in a kitchen. He and Orion had been working together at home, though, and Orion had been delighted to find out that Evan was actually good at baking. It had taken a bit of prodding on Davey's side, but Evan had eventually agreed to help Orion at the bakery. That meant that Orion didn't have to go to bed so late every night. He still woke up early, but he had time to rest during the afternoon because Evan was at the bakery then.

Which meant that Orion and Davey could spend more time together.

They had the house to themselves. They'd been watching a movie, but Orion had been sliding sideways almost since the first minute, and he'd snuggled against Davey's side, his face tucked against Davey's neck. He was breathing softly, and his entire body was relaxed, which told Davey everything he needed to know.

Orion trusted him enough to be with him like this. He

trusted him enough to fall asleep next to him. It felt good, but then, Davey's entire life felt good now.

The bakery was a success, and Orion had normal working hours. Evan was back, and he was living with Davey. They were getting used to being in each other's spaces again, and while Evan was dealing with everything that had happened to him, he'd taken the first step. It would take time for him to get over it—if he ever could—and he might not ever be the Evan that Davey had known, but that was okay. Davey had never expected him to be. He'd just wanted his friend back, and he had him.

He looked down. He also had Orion, whose eyes were blinking open.

Orion rolled away and stretched, his big body catching Davey's eye. Davey loved the way Orion looked, and he was attracted to his mate. Sometimes, it made things hard. Davey wanted sex with Orion, but he would never force Orion into something he was uncomfortable with. It was good that Orion didn't seem to mind when he noticed how interested Davey's body was, and he never teased. Davey truly didn't need sex. He didn't want it if Orion didn't, either. He dealt with his cock when it was unruly, and that was that. It wasn't a big thing between them or to Davey.

But there was something on Davey's mind, and it was a big thing. He wasn't quite sure how to broach the subject, though, so he continued watching Orion as he settled back on the couch next to him.

"What did I miss?" Orion asked, sounding sleepy.

"Almost the entire movie. It's probably best if you watch it again when you don't feel as tired."

Orion snuggled close. Davey buried his fingers in the hair at the back of Orion's neck and lightly scratched, smiling when Orion made a purr-like sound. Orion wasn't a shifter, but if he were one, he'd definitely be a cat.

"We'll try again tomorrow," Orion said. "Unless you don't want to watch it again since you didn't fall asleep."

"I can watch it again." Davey would do pretty much anything for Orion, so watching a movie twice wasn't a hardship.

He licked his lips. Davey wasn't sure he could wait any longer. He was going to explode if he didn't tell Orion what he was thinking.

"There's something I wanted to talk to you about," he said.

Orion sat up. "What is it? Did I do something you're not happy with?"

That was Orion's father speaking. The asshole had told Orion that he wasn't good enough and that he was an idiot so many times that Orion had started to believe him. Davey was working on showing him that wasn't the case, but it would take time for Orion to believe him. Davey had to fight against years of conditioning.

He was half tempted to go to the cells and strangle Mitchell. He doubted anyone would miss the guy, but Moore was still trying to get answers out of him, and Davey didn't want to mess that up. He doubted Moore would get those answers, but it was worth a try.

"No," Davey said before Orion could start freaking out too badly. "In fact, you've made me happy since the day we met."

Orion wrinkled his nose. "I don't think that's true."

"I'll be the judge of that, won't I?"

"What is it, then?"

"I was thinking about our bond. We haven't really talked about it, but I wouldn't be opposed to bonding with you."

For a moment, Orion was perfectly still. He stared at Davey with wide eyes, and Davey stared back because how could he not?

"You want to bond with me?" Orion asked.

"Yes."

"Even though we won't do it during sex?"

Davey almost rolled his eyes, but he understood why this was so important to Orion. From the little he'd said, he'd been made fun of and had been rejected a few times because he was asexual. Davey didn't understand why some people thought sex was so important in a relationship, but he didn't have to understand. To him, it didn't matter. What did matter was respect, love, and intimacy, and he and Orion had plenty of that. They didn't need to fuck to be in love or for their relationship to be perfect.

It was perfect for them.

"I don't care about that," Davey said as he leaned forward to kiss Orion's cheek. "And there's nothing I want more than to be bonded to you. I know it might feel like it's too fast, especially since you can't feel the bond, but I'd like you to think about it."

"Okay. I will." Orion paused and grinned. "Done. I want to bond with you."

Davey laughed. "Yeah?"

"I've been thinking about it, too. I was a bit hesitant, but I know that you don't care about the sex thing. I need to stop listening to the voice at the back of my head, especially since it sounds like my father."

Davey grimaced. "Please, never listen to whatever your father says."

"I'm working on it."

"That's all you can do." It would be enough, hopefully. Time away from his father would make everything easier for Orion.

"So how do we do this?" Orion asked.

Davey blinked. "You want to do it now?"

"No time like the present and all that, right?"

"I suppose." Davey looked around the living room. He could suggest they go upstairs, but he suspected Orion wouldn't be entirely comfortable with that. If the sex thing—

as Orion had said—had been on his mind, being anywhere near a bed wouldn't make him happy.

"We can do it here," Davey offered. "Or anywhere you're comfortable."

"I'm comfortable here."

He reached for Davey, making him squeak when he pulled him into his lap. Davey tilted his hips back because he didn't want Orion to feel how much he wanted him, but Orion pulled him forward again.

"You can move away if you're uncomfortable, but I don't mind feeling how much you want me," Orion murmured, cupping the back of Davey's head with one of his big hands. "Don't hide it from me. I might not want sex, but I do want to feel loved and desired."

Davey slumped forward, wrapping his arms around Orion's neck. He settled better in Orion's lap, straddling his thighs so he could face him.

He hesitated, then pushed closer, smiling when Orion's body relaxed. Davey did, too, because being wrapped around Orion like this felt like coming home.

Orion tilted his head to the side, and Davey pressed a kiss to the soft skin there. Orion smelled delicious and familiar, and being so close to him made Davey's wolf stir. Davey grinned at the sensation and kissed Orion's neck again. Orion squeezed his hips when Davey bit into his flesh.

Orion hugged Davey close, but he didn't restrict him. That meant that it was easy for Davey to reach for the side of his neck and slice it open with one claw.

Orion made a wounded sound, almost as if he was alarmed by the fact that Davey was hurt. Davey didn't stop sucking on the wound in Orion's neck, but he gently pulled Orion's face toward the cut he'd created. They needed to drink each other's blood if they wanted the bond to be complete.

Thankfully, Davey didn't have to explain what he wanted.

Orion obeyed his silent order and sealed his lips over his neck. He sucked strongly, sending a shiver down Davey's spine, but Davey ignored it and continued drinking.

Sometimes, he'd thought about how his bonding would go, and yes, he'd imagined it would happen during sex. This was perfect, though. In Orion's arms, he felt protected and loved, and that was all he could ever want.

When the bond snapped into place, it was almost as if Orion cradled Davey's being and tucked him around his heart to be cherished. Davey had never felt closer to anyone else, and he never would. He wouldn't want to.

Orion had been Davey's future before they'd even met, and now that they'd bonded, they would have decades together.

Davey couldn't wait.

ABOUT THE AUTHOR

Catherine is the creator of several series, most of them paranormal, including the Whitedell Pride Series and the Gillham Pack Series. While she graduated in translation, she decided to go the writer's way because it was more fun to create her own stories and characters.

She's been living in Italy for more than twenty years, but she's a daughter of the North—Belgium to be precise—and she misses it so much that she's already planning to move back.

She loves pizza—probably too much—her son, her pets, and of course, books. She sneaks some reading time into her schedule every time she has five minutes free from writing, demands from her various pets and son, and lastly, housework.

Connect with her:

lievens.catherine@gmail.com
BookBub: https://www.bookbub.com/authors/catherine-lievens
Website: https://authorcatherinelievens.com/
Facebook: https://www.facebook.com/catherine.lievens.9
Facebook Group: https://www.facebook.com/groups/411788002341528/
Twitter: https://twitter.com/authorCLievens
Newsletter: http://eepurl.com/c-uvKn

www.ingramcontent.com/pod-product-compliance
Lightning Source LLC
Chambersburg PA
CBHW060637130626
46555CB00002B/838